THE CRISTA 3 CHRONICLES

Robbers on Rock Road

Mark Littleton

HARVEST HOUSE PUBLISHERS
Eugene, Oregon 97402

ROBBERS ON ROCK ROAD

Copyright © 1993 by Mark Littleton
Published by Harvest House Publishers
Eugene, Oregon 97402

ISBN 1-56507-090-9

Library of Congress Catalog Card Number: 93-12716

Printed in the United States of America.

Contents

About the Author

Mark Littleton is the author of over 24 books, including the recent *Fillin' Up* in the Up Series of teen devotionals. He lives with his two children, Nicole and Alisha, in Columbia, Maryland.

·1·

Things to Think About

"I think I might do it," Crista Mayfield said to her sixth-grade friend, Jeff Pallaci, as they both gazed out over the still-frozen lake. It was a Saturday, no school. Late February. They sat on Jeff's grandfather's dock where it had been pulled up onto the beach for the winter. Crista mused, "She's really a nice kid and I know she wants to learn. Just having some trouble starting her reading, that's all."

Jeff, always fidgeting with something, drew back his slingshot and fired a pebble out onto the ice. "I think you'd be good at it, Crista."

"I would?" She felt surprised Jeff would compliment her like that. Not that Jeff wasn't decent about things. Crista thought of him as a good kid who was also scruffy enough to have fun. He had changed a lot since their first meeting when he was so obnoxious she almost told the police about him and his slingshot. But in the end they became close friends. She was pleased Jeff encouraged her.

"Yeah, you're good at that kind of stuff," Jeff answered. He began fitting another pebble into the sling pouch. "Watch this! It'll bounce all the way to the other side."

Crista watched as the stone arched upward, then struck the ice. It skittered across toward the other shore, about a half-mile away. Lake Wallenpaupack was 13 miles long, a manmade lake that had originally been the Paupack River. Over 50 years before, the State of Pennsylvania dammed up the river and created the lake. Crista and Jeff lived on a cove at the eastern end. Jeff's parents were in the middle of a divorce, so he was staying with his grandparents. Crista lived with her father, Dr. Jason Mayfield. He was an obstetrician—a doctor who delivers babies. Crista's mom had been killed in a car accident over a year ago.

Jumping down from the dock, Crista brushed snow off her jeans. Rontu, her milky white Great Dane, and Tigger, a Shelty and Rontu's ever-present partner, jumped up. The two dogs went just about everywhere Crista did. They had been lying under the dock while Jeff and Crista talked.

"What's her name?" Jeff said, pushing himself off the dock behind Crista.

"Lindy Helstrom," Crista answered. She bent down to tighten her figure skates. She and Jeff frequently skated together, even going as far as the small island about a mile down from their cove.

"What grade is she in?" Jeff asked. He began pulling on his skates, too.

"Second. Mrs. Walters. You know about her, don't you?"

"No."

"I had her in second grade too. She's very hard. She can really scare you the way she slaps down her ruler for quiet. And she has these big bulgy eyes." Crista frowned. "Well, maybe I shouldn't say that, but she does. Kids always talked about her bulgy eyes, even though it's not very nice...."

Jeff made a funny face. "Bulgy eyes? I think I saw her in a movie. It was called...What was it..."

Crista could tell Jeff was setting her up for a joke. "That's it. She was in *Night of the Bulgy-Eyed Teachers*."

Crista laughed. "Jeff, that's mean."

"Yeah, but I remember one of those teachers standing behind me, and her bulgy eyes dropped right onto my back. Kind of gooey."

"You're gross!" Crista gave him a shove. "Anyway, Mrs. Walters was good for me. I learned to keep my mouth shut when it should be shut, and also to listen to directions carefully."

"Leave it to you to turn *Night of the Bulgy-eyed Teachers* into *Mouths Shut and Ears Open for Second-Graders*."

Crista laughed, then jumped off the dock and ran down to the lake in her skates. "Race you to the point, meatball!"

"Meatball?!" Jeff yelled, as he dropped to the ground. "If I'm a meatball, you're a...a..."

"What's amatter? Can't think of a comeback?"

"Right," Jeff said, catching her. "You out-joked me once again."

Crista shook her head and stepped out onto the ice.

In three minutes, they were both panting and laughing after a hard race to the little jut of land that separated the end of the cove from the body of the lake. "Want to go to the island?" Jeff wheezed, as he grinned at Crista.

For once she'd beaten him, but Crista decided not to rub it in. Sometimes Jeff was sensitive about things like that.

They skated off leisurely toward the island, Rontu and Tigger trotting along behind them on the ice. As they loped along, bending slightly forward, their hands behind their backs, Jeff commented, "They still haven't caught the cabin-wreckers, have they?"

That winter, a number of summer cabins had been broken into and literally destroyed. Recently the authorities discovered that it wasn't just for fun or mischief, as they originally thought. Whoever the robbers were had been stealing video equipment, televisions, stereos, and anything else of value they could find in the cabins. They wrecked the first two or three because they hadn't found anything worth stealing in them. Most of the cabins on the lake were occupied only in the summertime, when their owners vacationed, boated, swam, and sailed on the lake. During the winter, the majority were empty, even though a few people—like Jeff's grandparents and Crista's father—remained on as residents.

"I haven't read anything about it lately."

"Yeah, I think the newspapers are toning it down," Jeff nodded. "They don't want to get too many people in an uproar."

"Have you heard something?"

"Just that two of the cabins on our side of the cove were broken into two weeks ago."

Crista turned to Jeff with a concerned look on her face. "Do you think they'd actually come to our section?"

"Well, you remember about Mrs. Holmes?" Jeff asked. "That's why I'm working on my aim with my slingshot."

Mrs. Holmes lived several doors down from Crista. Her home had been broken into, but since nothing had been stolen the police thought it was kids. In fact, some people had even accused Jeff, though he had not been involved.

Fixing her long brown hair under her ski cap, Crista answered, "Right, but they didn't steal anything from Mrs. Holmes."

"Should have."

"Well, if you didn't go around with that slingshot everywhere, people wouldn't think you were out shooting it into their lights and windows."

Jeff pulled it back and sent a stone clattering toward the point. "I should have been named Daniel Boone."

Jeff was good with the slingshot, even if Crista didn't approve of it the way Jeff wished she did. But she knew boys were like that, and if they were going to be friends, she had to give a little, too. Anyway, she knew very well stopping robbers with a slingshot was foolish, if not downright insane. Rumors had flown around that this "gang," however many there were of them, was a bunch of druggies who were financing their sick habits through robbing the houses. When they didn't find what they wanted, they tore the houses apart, even to the point of shooting bullets through lamps, refrigerators, ovens, and anything else that looked like an easy target. Crista knew some of it was just rumor, but it made her nervous at night, especially when her father was on call. Being an obstetrician meant his services might be needed at any hour of the day or night.

Crista, a shudder crackling through her chest and back, tried to sound casual. "What would you do if they really did come into one of our houses?" Crista trusted Jeff in ways she didn't trust other kids her age. He was reliable and loyal and definitely brave.

"Well, first, I'd get them in my sights," Jeff said, a little twinkle in his eye.

"Yeah?"

"Then I'd pull back my stone."

Crista rolled her eyes, expecting a joke. "Yeah?"

"Then I'd tell them to turn on the music."

"Turn on the music?"

"Yeah, and then I'd shoot them all. Call it rock music." Jeff's face lit up with a huge grin and Crista realized this was supposed to be a joke. He raised his eyebrows as he hit the laugh line. Crista only groaned.

As they neared the island, Crista noticed the air was slightly warmer and she sensed spring would be on their doorstep in less than a month. It was already the end of February. Usually by the end of March most of the snow would disappear and the ice would begin to melt. She liked winter and didn't want to see it go. Even with the shorter days and the chill, she loved the prickly feel of a frigid wind on her cheeks and the little spirals of air whisking snowflakes into a ballet across the ice.

After several minutes of silence, simply enjoying their glide across the lake toward the island, she said seriously, "No, really, Jeff. What would you do if they came to your house?"

He slowed down and stared at her with a curious look. "You're really worried about this, aren't you?"

She turned away from him. "Well, kind of." She didn't like admitting it, but it had given her the creeps lately. Her father repeatedly warned her to keep the doors locked, and Rontu and Tigger also made her feel safe. But over the last month, as the robberies moved closer to their part of the cove, she found herself worrying a lot.

"Hey," Jeff said quickly. "They won't go into an occupied house. Guaranteed. They don't want to get caught, and there are so many empty ones. Don't sweat it."

"But the empty ones don't have as much stuff as people who live up here year round." That was what really bothered her. She knew sooner or later the robbers would begin hitting the places more likely to have valuables. And those were the fulltime residents—like her, Jeff, and Mrs. Holmes.

"Look," Jeff was solemn. "What you do is call the police. 9-1-1. That's all I'd do. They'd be there in two minutes."

"I don't think so."

"Five minutes."

"Just enough for a robber to strangle me."

Jeff glanced at her anxiously. "They're not coming around you, Crista, believe me."

"Why?"

"Because of me!" Jeff's face lit up again. "Those robbers wouldn't want to have to deal with me, that's for sure."

Giving Jeff a playful shove, Crista skated on toward the island. She told herself not to think about it anymore. She did have Rontu and Tigger and both of them were fighters, when it was called for. So what was there to worry about? And Jeff was right. Calling the police was the first step in any emergency like that. She wondered how soon someone would invent a belt phone you could have with you all the time!

· 2 ·
Lindy

That Tuesday, Crista had her first chance to tutor Lindy Helstrom. They both jumped off the yellow school bus that stopped at the top of Rock Road where the Helstroms' house stood. They lived down past the Wilkinses' farm, friends of Crista's who owned several horses.

They walked down to the house from the highway. When they reached the brick walkway up to it, three gray cats scampered out, arching their backs and purring.

"This is Baloney, Cheese, and Hot Dog," Lindy introduced her pets. She wore thick glasses and usually cocked her head when listening, as if she didn't quite hear all you were saying.

"Were they born inside of sandwiches?" Crista asked, bending down to pet one of them, not sure who was who at the moment. The hefty one looked like the mother and sure enough, Lindy said, "That's Cheese. She's the mother of the other two." Cheese was a light reddish-gray with patches of white and black. Hot Dog and Baloney had different white and gray markings. Lindy explained, "Baloney is the one with the white tip on her tail. And Hot Dog has the dark gray booties."

13

Lindy and Crista ambled down the brick inlaid path. Crista gazed up at the house with wonder and also a little nervousness. It was large—at least twice as big as her cabin—and tall, with funny-looking towers on both ends that reminded her of buildings she'd seen in pictures of Russia. A huge porch ran all the way around the front and sides. It was white, with a green-shingled roof and a latticed railing around the edge. There was a garage in the back. It was one of those houses that Crista suspected would look as if it were haunted, especially at night.

"Come on, I'll show you my room." Lindy took her by the hand and pulled her forward.

Crista obediently followed her newest responsibility. Lindy's mother had asked the guidance counselor at Wallenpaupack Elementary, Mrs. Breck, if someone might be able to spend time with Lindy and tutor her, and also do a little babysitting. The Helstroms owned a restaurant down the lake called "Country Picnics" that was always crowded and served the best fried chicken and fried clam platters in the area. At least, that was the way it was advertised. The two or three times Dr. Mayfield had taken Crista there, she believed it was probably true. Even her own mother had not made fried chicken like theirs.

Mr. and Mrs. Helstrom spent a lot of time before lunch and dinner at the restaurant, so Lindy had been in day care, but she hated it. After meeting Mrs. Helstrom the week before and talking about the assignment, Crista agreed to come up at least two afternoons a week. She would stay from 3:30 to 7:00 to play with Lindy, tutor her, and just be a friend. The other days for Lindy were split up between day care and hanging around the restaurant. Crista had responsibilities at home that meant she couldn't do it five days a week, even though she would have liked to.

The Helstroms would pay her, too. That was the best part. Ten dollars a day! Enough maybe to buy her own horse in a year or so. Or perhaps a new set of skates. Crista could think of a million things she'd like to buy now that she would have some money of her own to spend. And save, too.

She and Lindy stopped in front of the door. Lindy pointed to the floor. "Guess where?"

Mrs. Helstrom had told Crista where to find the key—under a board on the porch by the front mat—and Lindy obviously knew, but she liked playing games so Crista went along. Crista scrutinized the floor boarding, but it all looked the same to her.

Lindy turned to her. "Give up?"

Nodding her head, Crista said, "It's hidden really well."

Lindy bent down and pushed a small board at one end. Immediately, it sprang up.

"One of my dad's little inventions," she beamed proudly.

It was a good thing Lindy knew what to do, Crista thought. The board was so well concealed that no one would have suspected it. But when it flipped up, the tiny hiding place was revealed.

Crista slid the key into the hole in the doorknob, then tried to turn it. But it didn't move.

"You have to jiggle it around a little," Lindy instructed.

Crista moved the key back and forth slightly in the hole, putting pressure so that it would turn when it moved into the proper place. In a moment, it turned and the door opened.

They stepped into a fashionable house. These people are rich! Crista thought. A shiny walnut split table sat in the entryway, with one side flipped up against the wall and the other flat with a lamp, a pile of mail, and some knickknacks that looked expensive on it.

Lindy led Crista to a spacious kitchen in the back. It had a large refrigerator, an island with a cutting board on top, and a copper-colored range. But Crista's interest led her to the sink. Antique, ivory-colored, with large brass spigots and handles, it was something Crista remembered her mother had always wanted for their cabin. "This is beautiful!" Crista ran her fingers along the rim.

"Yeah, my mom found it about a year ago. She said she's been looking for one for about a hundred years." Lindy flashed her wide smile. Her red hair and freckles made her look pixie-ish. She was definitely not as shy as Crista had been led to believe. Lindy crackled with fun and her smile was wider than Jeff's, whom Crista thought had one of the best smiles she'd ever seen on a boy.

Taking off her coat, Crista draped it over one of the roundback farm chairs clustered about the large oak kitchen table. They walked through the family room off the kitchen. Again, it was filled with antique furniture, rich wooden sitting chairs and end tables, two velvet-covered couches and a loveseat, and a rolltop desk in one corner. Crista marveled as she gazed at the large television screen about the size of the side of a barn.

Then she noticed a stereo tower with monstrous speakers hung on four walls, and even an electric guitar set up on a stand with an amplifier. Crista said with awe, "Who plays the guitar?"

"My dad," Lindy replied.

"Is he good?"

"I guess." Lindy turned around and looked at her. "Want to hear it?"

"Well, not if you're not allowed or something."

"Oh, I'm allowed." Lindy picked up the instrument and hit a switch on the amp. A sharp buzzing sound filled the air. On the floor was a little footpad with about eight switches. Crista had never seen one, and under each push button was a little piece of plastic tape with a word. "Reverb," "fuzz," "bass-boom," "vibrato," and "wah-wah" among them, names she didn't know the meaning of.

"My dad was in a rock band before he met my mom," Lindy said. She picked up a cord and jammed it into a plughole on the bottom half of the guitar. "It's a Fender," she explained. "Ever heard of Fender?"

"No."

"Telecaster." She pointed to the name in pearl at the top of the neck. "It's the kind a lot of famous rock stars use. That's what Daddy says, anyway."

Crista wondered what Jeff would do if he saw all this. He'd go nuts, she knew. He was always talking about being a rock star when he grew up.

Lindy grinned at her mischievously. "Ready for the blast?"

Swallowing, Crista asked, "Should I cover my ears?"

"No. Just listen." She plucked the bass string with a white pick she took off the top of the amplifier. Instantly, the room filled with sound. It was loud, but somehow thrilling.

"Now listen to this," Lindy said. She touched the string, stopping it from vibrating, then pressed one of the switches with her foot. Immediately, a strange electric noise resounded and she banged the string again. This time it was fuzzy-sounding. Lindy talked over the sound, "That's the fuzz-tone. Ever hear a song on the radio with a sound like that?"

Crista knew she had and she nodded her head. She also knew, though, she'd have to take charge real quick, or Lindy would have them messing around all afternoon when they were supposed to be working on her homework.

"All right, let's get down to the reading before we forget."

Lindy lifted the guitar over her shoulders, then turned off the amp. "I'm glad you're here," she said.

"You are?" Crista was surprised by Lindy's blunt honesty.

"Yeah. I get scared sometimes." Lindy's eyes grew concerned.

"You do?"

"Well, you know. Those bad guys have been breaking in and wrecking houses in the neighborhood." Lindy took a look around the family room. "I hope they don't come here."

"Oh, they won't," Crista reassured the little girl.

But she wasn't as confident on the inside as she sounded. If the cabin-wreckers knew what the Helstroms had, they'd be here in no time!

Lindy led Crista to the back of the house where her bedroom was. "Mommy and Daddy sleep next door and I do here, but we also have four bedrooms upstairs, too. But they don't heat it up there real well to save money. So we're all on the main floor."

She turned the old-fashioned roundhole key. "My mom likes old-timey stuff," Lindy said, pointing to the key and taking it out. "Every door has one." She put it back in the keyhole. Crista stepped in behind Lindy and looked around. The walls were lined with shelves and a horde of stuffed animals, pictures, books, dolls, games, and everything else any little girl could want. In one corner was a little rocking chair that had to be a hundred years old. She had a canopy bed with dangly white tassels all around the upper edge. The bed was covered in what looked like a giant doily with a quilt underneath and several large pillows at the head.

"It was my mom's when she was little," Lindy said, obviously noticing Crista looking at it with awe.

The bed sat in the middle of the room, and on the other side Lindy showed Crista a large black iron grate. "For the heat," she explained. "But it comes off." She gave Crista a mysterious, confidential look. "They're all over the house." She leaned down to show her and started to pull it off.

But Crista stopped her. "All right, Lindy. We have to do some reading and math, remember?"

Sighing with frustration, Lindy complained, "I can't get away with anything."

"I think you get away with everything." Crista gave her a little push toward the bedroom door. "If we don't do a half-hour of reading and a half-hour of math, your mother will have both our heads."

"Not heads," Lindy said brightly. "Our ears. She has a collection."

Crista wrinkled her nose with disgust.

Lindy laughed. "I can trick you so easy!"

Shaking her head with amusement, Crista walked over to the shelf of books and looked through them. "Anything you want to read real bad?"

Immediately, Lindy's face turned dark. Clearly, this was one thing she wouldn't enjoy, and Crista realized for all Lindy's excitement about guitars and cats and heat grates, reading was one thing she had a rough time with. Crista chose a book she knew was easy, one of those funny long poem-stories by Dr. Seuss. She led Lindy back into the family room.

"We'll go through this first," she said in a commanding tone.

Lindy followed her out, her enthusiasm dampened. Crista sensed this was going to be one long road.

·3·

Fast Car

Lindy struggled through the first page of the poem. When she was finished, Crista made her read it again. Still, she stumbled over several words. They repeated the process four times before they moved on to page two. Lindy looked embarrassed and tense.

"Just relax," Crista finally said. "I'm not grading you on this."

"I know," Lindy answered with frustration. "I'm just dumb."

"You are not dumb!"

"Everybody at school says I am."

"Everybody?"

Lindy looked down into her lap. She hunched over and her pigtails draped down over her shoulders. "Everybody," she muttered without looking up.

Crista knew this tactic. She'd used it herself enough times. Usually, though, it came down to maybe one or two or three kids who razzed her. It seemed like everybody sometimes, but fortunately it was rarely that bad. "Name them," she said to Lindy.

"Marcie and Autumn and..."

There was a long pause. Crista prompted, "And?"

"And...and...I don't know." Lindy bunched her

fist and smashed it onto the face of the book. "I don't know all the names."

"Yes you do."

Crista could see she was near tears. She put her arm around Lindy's shoulders. "All right, so it's a couple of kids. Forget them. Be friends with someone else."

"I don't want to be friends with anyone else."

Sighing, Crista said, "Well, what do they say? What do they do that makes you feel they think you're dumb?"

This was a process Crista had gone through probably a thousand times with her own mother when she was in first and second grade. She'd had a hard time, too. But in the end she began to learn that few things in life went the way you wished they did. Many kids found reading difficult. And the ones who didn't have a tough time often made it tough on others.

"They laugh when I have to read out loud," Lindy pouted.

"They do?"

"Yeah, and they snicker."

"Well, aren't there other girls to be friends with?"

Lindy suddenly turned her head and looked into Crista's eyes. "You."

Crista smiled. "Of course, me. Anytime you see me, I'm there, okay?" She held up her fist and Lindy stared at it. "Punch my fist with yours," she said.

Lindy made a fist and tapped Crista's.

"That's what we do to show we're friends. My mom used to do that with me all the time," Crista explained.

"That's neat," Lindy said. "Let's do it again."

Crista shook her head. "Once is enough. Now let's get back to that reading."

They spent the next hour chugging away. Then they worked on addition and subtraction. Lindy battled the numbers like a gladiator, but she seemed unable to grasp some of the most basic concepts.

When they finished, it was past five o'clock and dark outside. Mrs. Helstrom was supposed to get home about seven and drive Crista back down to her cabin. They had more than an hour to do something else, so Crista suggested, "Want to take a walk?"

Lindy instantly jumped up. "Yeah, let's. In the dark. Cool."

They dressed in their thick ski parkas and went outside, making sure to lock the front door. Lindy had a flashlight. Crista said, "We can just go up the road aways and see what's there to see."

"Yeah!" Lindy yelled, punching the air with her fist.

They started up the blacktop to the right as they came out of the Helstroms' driveway. There were large patches of snow by the road in piles. The plows came through after a snow and heaped it up like that so it often remained unmelted till spring. The woods, though, were still covered. Many of the trees hung down from the weight of the snow on their branches.

"Do you know the names of the trees?" Crista asked as they walked along.

"No," Lindy said. "I've always wondered."

"Okay, I'll tell you. We'll have a little test. And maybe in school you can really show up those two girls who laugh at you. You do study trees in second grade. In fact it should be coming up. I remember."

"All right!" Lindy cried enthusiastically.

Crista took the flashlight and shone it in among the trees. Catching the black and white coloring of a paper birch, she stopped and pointed to it. She explained its name and then moved on to others—elm, red maple, maple, poplar, fir tree, and others. She showed Lindy the different barks and how the leaves—when she could find a few dead brown ones on the ground— looked, or how the needles were shaped on the pines. She gave Lindy a quick test. In a matter of minutes, the little girl memorized the names. Crista wondered if Lindy would learn to read faster than others thought since she could grasp this so easily.

After exploring in the woods for a few more minutes, Crista checked her watch and realized they'd better get back. It was getting close to seven. They returned to the road and started up the blacktop toward Lindy's house.

A minute later, two headlamps appeared ahead of them. Crista could already hear the whoosh of the car or truck, gravel hurtling out behind the tires. She grabbed Lindy by the upper arm and pulled her over onto one of the piles of snow.

Turning to look, she said, "This guy is really moving."

"The weirdos," Lindy commented tightly.

"The weirdos?"

"They live down that way..." She pointed past her house.

The truck was close to their side of the road. Crista pulled Lindy back, then started to lose her balance.

The truck ripped by in a spray of snow, gravel, sand, and whipping wind. There were two men in it with cowboy hats on. Both girls fell over backwards, tumbling over the other side of the snow mound.

"Good grief!" Crista yelled as she watched the truck continue on around the bend. "Who do they think they are? They could have run us down!"

"Yeah, they're always tearing along around here," Lindy said angrily as she stood and brushed the snow off her hat and pants. "They think this is a race course."

"Who are they?" Crista asked, climbing up to the top of the mound to look. When she saw the brake lights go on and the wheels squeal to a halt, she slid down the bank.

"They live up the road in an old cabin," Lindy answered.

"They shouldn't drive like that. They could have hit us!"

"Yeah, my dad always says to stay off the road when I'm walking on it, or riding my bike."

"Good idea. Let's get home."

Suddenly, a voice called out behind them. "Hey! Hey, you two?"

Prickles ran up Crista's back. She turned around and saw a scraggly looking guy in a leather jacket, cowboy hat, and boots walking toward them.

·4·

Cruz

Crista wasn't sure whether to run or wait. They were in sight of the Helstroms' house, but no one was home.

Then the man called out, "Hey, I'm really sorry. My friend Rick drives a little crazy."

Crista didn't answer as the stumpy guy walked up to them. She kept the flashlight shining on the ground, but she could see his face. The truck sat in the road well behind them, not moving.

"I'm really sorry," he apologized again as he stepped into the circle of light. "I keep telling Rick there are kids around here. My name is Cruz." He held out his hand.

Not sure what to think or say, Crista took it and shook it. She introduced herself and Lindy to Cruz. Then she said, "You really scared us."

Cruz had a guilty, sheepish look on his face. "Yeah, we weren't expecting to see someone on the road like that. Rick . . . well, he's a wild man in that truck of his."

"You live in the falling-down house," Lindy stated matter-of-factly.

Cruz laughed. He had brown skin and brown eyes and dark, black hair. He had dealt with Crista's first bad impression rather well. "We'll be more careful, I

27

promise you," he said. "Now that we know you'll be around."

"Thanks." Crista still wasn't sure how talk to this guy, but he seemed harmless, even if his friend drove like a maniac.

Backing up, Cruz tipped his hat, then nodded his head. "Be seeing you. Thanks for accepting my apology. I will get Rick to simmer down, I promise."

"Thanks," Crista repeated.

She and Lindy watched Cruz walk back to his truck. Twice he stopped, turned around, and waved. Finally, he opened the door and they drove off.

"His friend mustn't be real nice," Lindy said as they turned back to the house.

"You should give everyone a chance until they prove otherwise," Crista pointed out.

"You should?"

"Something my dad says. And another one: 'People surprise you. Every day.'"

"That's true." Lindy nodded.

Listening, Crista noticed the whir of the wind. The woods, though, were quiet now. Only the occasional pitter-patter of a squirrel broke the silence. She loved this time of night in the woods. It never scared her, even though she knew there were scary things in the woods at night. Somehow it gave her a peaceful feel-ing.

Lindy suddenly cried, "Let's race!"

She was off before Crista had a chance to answer. The slap of Lindy's boots on the blacktop resounded in the quiet woods. Crista dug in and sprinted after her, yelling at her to keep to the side of the road. Lindy was barreling nearly up the middle. If Rick and his truck came back, she was done for.

Crista was fast, though, and soon caught up. "Lindy, get out of the middle of the road!" she said, jostling her by the collar.

Lindy slowed down. "Sorry. I forgot."

They both stopped and began to walk on the side. "How could you forget so quickly?"

"I don't know," Lindy shrugged her shoulders. "You think I'm dumb, don't you?"

"No, I don't think you're dumb. I think you're not being careful enough. That truck could run you right down. My mom was killed that way."

Lindy stared at her. "Your mom?"

For a moment, it choked Crista up. But gaining control of her emotions, she told Lindy how her mother had been killed by a drunk driver. "We were both walking down the sidewalk in town. And then a man just came around the corner. It was over in seconds."

Lindy was very quiet. When Crista finished, she said, "I'm sorry. I didn't know."

"It's all right," Crista pushed back the lump in her throat. "I just don't want to see that happen to you."

"It won't," Lindy said bluntly. "I will be more care-ful."

Crista took her mittened hand and squeezed it. "Come on, let's run again and stick to the side."

They were both off and in a few minutes stood on the porch of the huge house.

·5·

Portrait

"Oh, look! There's the dum-dum!"

Crista and Jeff turned from where they had been waiting in the bus yard to see who was shouting so loudly. Immediately, Crista noticed Lindy walking toward them, her face clouded over. Behind her a bigger girl followed closely, a smirk on her face. Crista recognized her as Autumn Bramo-something.

"Bye, dum-dum!" the bigger girl taunted as she passed Lindy and headed out of the yard.

When Lindy reached Crista and Jeff, she looked ready to burst into tears. Crista started to say something, but Lindy just brushed by her angrily. "Don't say anything to me," she muttered between clenched teeth. "Anything!"

Crista turned to Jeff and sighed. "I have to do something to cheer her up."

"Yeah, like what?"

"I don't know. I'll think of something."

The three of them rode the bus home in silence. By the time they reached their stop and hopped off, Crista had her plan figured out.

"Hey, you guys, why don't we stop at my place before we go to the Helstroms'?" she asked, trying not to sound too enthusiastic.

"Well, okay," Jeff agreed hesitantly. "As long as I get to see the guitar sometime today." Jeff had been pestering Crista the whole weekend about coming along to the Helstroms' as soon as he found out about the Fender.

"We still have to call Mrs. Helstrom and see if it's okay for you to come over," Crista reminded him. "Lindy?" she tapped the little girl on the arm. "Is it okay with you if we stop by my house?"

"Whatever," Lindy shrugged.

When they reached the Mayfields' house, Crista led everyone inside and called. Someone named Nancy answered, but Mrs. Helstrom came on a moment later.

"Yes, Crista." Mrs. Helstrom had a slight German accent.

"I was wondering if a friend of mine might come up to the house this afternoon," Crista said, looking at Jeff and raising her eyebrows. "He's from my class." She explained who Jeff was and how they knew each other.

"All right," Mrs. Helstrom replied briskly. "But make sure Lindy does her homework."

"I will," Crista promised.

"Good. We'll see you at seven. Take you both home."

"There's one more thing."

"Yes?"

"I was planning to do something for Lindy." She dropped her voice to a whisper, "A portrait, but I have to do it here at my house."

Mrs. Helstrom hesitated, then said, "Okay, but get up to the house before it's dark."

"Okay!"

Hanging up, Crista nodded to Jeff and then turned to Lindy and said mysteriously, "You need to sit in that chair." She pointed to one of the kitchen chairs.

"What is this?" Lindy asked. She was obviously curious, but she obeyed Crista's instruction.

Crista set up the easel. She planned to do the portrait in charcoal. She had been learning to work in that medium for the last month from her art teacher, Mr. Falkland.

"What is this?" Lindy asked again.

"You'll see!"

Crista positioned Lindy and then switched on the spotlight she'd gotten that winter to beam direct light on Lindy's face. Jeff had gone into the living room and was playing something by a country western singer Crista's father liked.

"Sit real still and look off above the refrigerator," Crista instructed, "like you're looking at beautiful deer in the woods."

Lindy said, "How about a fox? I like foxes."

"Okay, a fox." Crista grinned. She began the drawing, making a few light lines to outline Lindy's face, hair, and neck. In about five minutes, she had the basic shapes down.

Lindy suddenly announced, "You're drawing a picture of me!"

"Just wait and you'll see." Crista smiled.

Impatiently swinging her legs as she sat on the chair, Lindy looked around the kitchen. Crista kept telling her to smile "like for the camera" or "like it was Christmas morning and you just opened the best present you ever saw."

"A softball, bat, and glove," Lindy said. "That would be the best."

"Oh, you like softball? You never told me that."

"I haven't told you a lot of things."

"Like what?" Crista drew quickly but carefully, shading in the dark spots under Lindy's chin and on the far side of her face. She rubbed the charcoal with her index finger, spreading the gray in different blends and hues. Jeff cranked the stereo up rather high. The house was vibrating.

Lindy shouted over the music, "Like my guinea pig, Herbert."

"Your guinea pig?"

"Yeah, I have a guinea pig. He stays down in the basement. I'll show him to you today if you want."

"Okay. What else?" Crista called to the living room. "Jeff! Turn it down. My father'll kill us."

The music sank down a notch and Crista frowned with exasperation. "You'd think he was completely deaf," she said to Lindy. But Lindy only smiled as if she knew something Crista didn't.

"I'm good at finding neat hiding places," Lindy got a michievous grin on her face. "Like in hide-and-seek. No one ever finds me."

"Where do you hide?"

"It's a secret. I can only tell you when you're on my team."

Crista pretended to be hurt, but Lindy didn't budge. She said, "If I told you all my hiding places, then you'd know and you'd catch me and you'd win. And I can't let that happen."

"Just wait till you play with Jeff sometime. He'll find you."

"Never."

"Okay, we'll see." Crista smiled and sketched in the last elements of the picture, Lindy's eyes and mouth.

Jeff walked into the kitchen, looked at the drawing and whistled. Crista said, "Know what that is?"

Jeff peered at the picture. "Lindy."

"Yes, but what about that?" She pointed to a creature sitting in Lindy's lap. It was a caricature drawing, with Lindy's head full size, but her body underneath tiny and even funny.

"I don't know."

"Come here, Lindy. Tell Mr. Know It All what's on your lap."

Lindy hurried over to the easel. She stared at the drawing, then yelled, "It's Herbert! My little guinea pig. And I have on a baseball glove with a bat over my shoulder! Wow, am I pretty!"

Crista grinned. "I learned to do that from Mr. Falkland. He does caricatures at the mall sometimes."

"It looks just like me." Lindy was amazed. Crista had decked Lindy out in long pigtails with blue ribbons. Little baseballs and bats shone out on each ribbon.

"You never drew me like that," Jeff mused.

"That's because you can never sit still," Crista teased. She sprayed a special "fixing" solution onto the charcoal drawing so it wouldn't smudge, then waited for it to dry.

Lindy couldn't take her eyes off the picture. "I bet no one in second grade has anything like this!" she proclaimed happily.

"Why don't you show it to them?" Crista asked.

"Could I?"

"Sure. It's yours. You can do whatever you want with it."

Lindy gave Crista a big hug. "It's the best present I ever got! Thanks, Crista."

"You're very welcome." Crista was glad her plan to cheer up Lindy had worked.

"When are you going to do me?" Jeff insisted. He was obviously impressed, as he usually was when Crista drew while he watched. "How can you do that?"

"Talent," Crista joked. "And beauty, riches. All that stuff."

"Yeah, right," Jeff said. He continued gazing at the picture with awe. "She's really good, isn't she, Lindy? I've never seen anyone who could draw like her. You think she'll be an artist if she grows up?"

"If?" Crista questioned immediately.

"If!" Jeff said and raised his eyebrows dramatically. "No, not 'if.' I'll say, 'She might be a great artist if she could grow up, but since she can't...'"

Crista gave him a quick slug on the upper arm. Jeff recoiled with mock pain. "Oh, she's a boxer, too!"

Shaking her head with pretend disgust, Crista handed the picture to Lindy. Immediately, Lindy said, "You didn't sign it."

"Oh, yes I did," Crista replied right away. "You'll just have to find it. Hide-and-seek. See if I'm better at this than you."

Lindy looked over the picture and Jeff bent over behind her, both of them looking for Crista's signature. They were about to give it up, when Lindy spotted it on the label of the bat over her shoulder. Crista had etched it in almost invisibly.

"There it is!" Lindy cried. She pointed to it and Jeff grinned.

"Not bad," he nodded. "I couldn't find it."

"When I'm famous, they'll say I always put my name somewhere special!" Crista waited for both of them to laugh. "Like Vincent Van Gogh did."

"Who's he?" Lindy asked.

Crista rolled her eyes. "Only the most famous artist in history, after Michelangelo and Picasso."

"Who are they?" Jeff gave Lindy and Crista his monkey face.

Crista pushed them all out into the living room. "Get your coats on now, people, or we'll be late, and I'll lose my job and end up a bag lady."

"Yes, sir!" Jeff said, giving a salute.

Crista helped Lindy pull her coat on and as they went to the door, she said, "Now we've got to get to that tutoring, or your mom'll be upset."

After they were all ready, the three of them marched up the road toward the highway. Rontu and Tigger followed along behind them. Mrs. Helstrom had told Crista the dogs could stay on the porch, but they were not to come into the house. Lindy carried the picture rolled up in her backpack and promised to ask her mom to frame it and hang it up in her bedroom—after she took it to school.

As they walked up the road, Jeff took out a penknife and began carving a stick. Crista and Lindy threw snowballs at trees. The snow was icy. It had been melting for the past few days, and even the lake looked bright and wet in the sun. It was just a warm spell, though, and would probably pass.

When they finally reached Lindy's house, it was twilight. Jeff immediately wanted to see the guitar. Lindy obediently showed him, then turned it on and let him pluck the strings with the guitar still on the stand. As it resounded throughout the house, Lindy took Crista down into the basement so she could meet Herbert. Rontu and Tigger stayed out on the porch.

The cats walked about, darting in and out of the trees and shrubbery.

The little guinea pig was brown with a ruff of white around his shoulders. Lindy caressed the little beast's fur and lifted him out of the cage. Then she let Crista hold him. He was soft, didn't bite, and even "chirped" a couple times. Lindy immediately said, "He likes you."

"Oh, does he?" Crista raised her eyebrows. "How do you know?"

"I can tell. I told him he had to anyway, so I guess he's just obeying me."

Crista laughed and gave the chirping guinea pig a kiss, then began to set him back in the cage. Suddenly, Lindy yelled, "Hide-and-seek. Hide-and-seek. Bet you can't find me!"

She scurried up the stairs, leaving Crista with Herbert still in her hand. She gently placed him back in his cage, and ran up the stairs, shouting that it was time to do the tutoring, but Lindy had disappeared. Crista walked into the family room where Jeff was staring at the guitar and trying different foot switches, then vibrating a string to see what it would sound like.

"Jeff, no playing with the guitar. We agreed to that."

Jeff gave her a repentant look. "It's just so cool."

"It'll have to be cool while you're on the other side of the room. I mean it."

"Okay."

"Where'd Lindy go?"

"I haven't seen her."

"Ugh!" Crista moaned. "We'll never get any work done. From now on it's homework first and nothing else, no matter what."

·6·

A Scare

Crista called at the top of her lungs, "Lindy, get down here this minute! I'm not kidding now!"

There was no answer. Crista and Jeff stood in the foyer, looking up the stairs and into the different rooms around them. "Where could she have gone to?" Frustration edged Crista's voice.

"Guess she wants us to find out," Jeff said.

"Turn off the guitar and let's find her," Crista said, her frustration turning to anger.

"Oh, come on," Jeff tried to lighten things up. "She's just having a little fun."

"I have a job to do here, Jeff. This is not just fun."

"Okay, all right. Let's just find her then. Who knows, maybe we'll also find a werewolf or the headless horseman or Indiana Jones or somebody."

Crista sighed unhappily. "You look down here, I'm going upstairs. Check Lindy's room first." She stomped up the stairs, making as much noise as she could and yelling, "When I find you, Lindy, it's gonna be bad!"

The rooms upstairs were eerie and quiet. With the guitar turned off and only the faint sound of Jeff whistling downstairs, Crista's scalp prickled with fear. There were some guest rooms, Lindy had told her. But she hadn't said anymore about it. A slightly musty smell snagged Crista's nostrils. Plenty of doors and closets appeared as she scanned each room. One was a sewing room. Another had weights in it and a walking machine. Crista hurried through them, talking to herself and the walls, hoping Lindy would get the message and just come back. But there were no sounds, not even the muffled laughing Crista expected Lindy to be doing while Crista walked by her hiding place for the tenth time.

When Crista was sure she'd tried everywhere, she stood at the door to the attic. She opened it a crack, looked in. It was absolutely dark, and she was certain Lindy would not hide up there in the dark like that. She called, "Lindy, if you're up there, I'm not coming up. So you'd just better come on down." She waited for an answer, but there was none. "Ugh! Where is she? Her mother is going to hang me first and then her!"

Finally finding a light switch, Crista mounted the creaking stairs. A dry dusty smell made her sneeze. If the top floor had been eerie, the attic was positively creepy. She stepped carefully, stopping on each step before going on and listening. Her heart was pounding. What could be up there?

A moment later, she heard a sound behind her. She jumped, almost falling backwards. It was Jeff.

"I can't find her," he said simply.

"You almost gave me a heart attack!" Crista replied angrily. This was getting to her now and she didn't like it. "Come on, let's look up here and if we don't find her, we're going downstairs to sit and wait. I'm not spending the whole afternoon playing games."

Jeff was behind her. She turned and looked at him. "Aren't you going first?"

"Me?" Jeff asked with wide eyes. "I'm not that brave."

Setting her teeth grimly, Crista pressed forward, not stopping now or pausing. "Just what I need, a bunch of scaredy cats."

Jeff only grinned and poked her. "Just want to see how really tough you are."

"Ugh!"

Soon they stood in the main part of the attic. It was gigantic. Everywhere clothing, furniture, paintings, and a multitude of things Crista couldn't even begin to describe stood in all kinds of positions, piles, and hangings. Instantly, though, Crista envisioned what great fun to sift through everything and maybe find something unusual.

She called, "Lindy, if you're up here, come out, come out wherever you are."

Waiting, Jeff poked her again in the side. She jumped, then whipped around. "Jeff!" She glared at him. "This is serious. I'm supposed to be tutoring her, not playing hide-and-seek."

They stalked up the aisles in the attic, looking under the drop cloths that covered some of the furniture and peering around in the corners where the eaves of the roof came together with the main part of the building.

"She's not here," Crista finally said. "And if she is, we can't find her."

"Let's just go all the way to the end."

Crista peered down the long flat path of boards that formed the main aisle. A webwork of beams and poles jutted here and there at odd angles, obviously holding up the roof.

When they reached the end, they both peered out the window into the driveway below. They had to be up at least 30 feet. Crista sighed, "Well, I guess we have to give up."

They turned around. Suddenly, the lights went out.

"Lindy!" Crista screamed.

No answer.

They heard something coming up the steps.

"Linnnnnn-deeeeeee!" Crista was really scared now. What if someone had gotten into the house? What if it wasn't Lindy?

She felt out in front of her for something familiar. Her hand brushed on and then grasped coats and furniture. She stumbled forward. "Jeff! Jeff! Where are you?"

"Right behind you." She felt his breath on her neck. "What is going on?"

"I don't know."

The boards ahead of them creaked. Something was coming down toward them. Crista's heart seemed to be booming right through the roof. Fighting the tremor in her voice, she said, "If that's you, Lindy, tell me. I do not like this. Repeat, I do not..."

Suddenly, a flashlight went on. Immediately, Crista's eyes focused on something low and ugly, a hairy face with fangs! It roared and leaped at them.

Crista screamed. Jeff fell against her. The thing advanced. Then Jeff pushed Crista out of the way and grabbed it. The thing squealed with pain. It was Lindy!

Ripping off a monster mask that looked half were-wolf, half grizzly bear, Lindy screeched with pleasure. "Got you all!"

Jeff had tumbled into the coats after grabbing Lindy and knocking her flashlight to the floor, but the little girl was beaming. Crista blinked, trying to calm herself and still the pounding in her chest. She could hardly breathe! "Lindy!" she wheezed. "What are you..."

"Were you scared? Were you really scared?"

Jeff jumped up, brushing himself off. "Yes, I was scared!"

Lindy only grinned. "I did it to my cousin, Lewie, at Christmas, and he ran out of the attic screaming and howling. It was great!"

"Lindy," Crista said, pulling her up to her feet. "Get out of that costume and let's go do some reading and math."

"Oh, do we have to? This is more fun."

Giving Jeff a frustrated look, Crista led Lindy down the corridor. "Your mother is getting a full report, little girl."

Instantly, Lindy wheeled around, a look of terror on her face. "Oh, please. Please don't tell her. Please. I was just kidding."

"We'll see." Feeling finally triumphant, Crista winked at Jeff. They all clopped out of the attic to the main floor, then down the stairs. When they reached the bottom, Crista asked, "Were you hiding, or were you preparing the whole time for your little scare thing?"

Lindy shook her head. "I was hiding the whole time. But then I heard Jeff go upstairs, and I knew you were in the attic, so I just had to get out my Halloween outfit."

"Where were you hiding?" Crista wanted to know.

Lindy shook her head. "My secret. I can't tell, or then you'll know my best place."

Giving Jeff a hard look, Crista said, "All right, we'll let it go this time. But no more hide-and-seek, got it?"

"Got it!" Lindy grinned from Crista to Jeff. They went into the family room after Lindy took off the monster suit and worked again at the reading and then at the math. Lindy still was not making progress. She stumbled over the same words repeatedly and missed simple addition problems in math. All the same, Crista could see she was trying. Maybe she was just trying to make up for the scare, but the little girl did inspire some real respect the way she dug in and gave it her best attempt.

When Mrs. Helstrom arrived at seven to take them home, she let both Crista and Jeff off at Jeff's house. Rontu and Tigger jumped out the back of the Helstroms' station wagon. As the car drove off, Crista said, "She's really not making much progress, Jeff. What can we do?"

Jeff watched the car disappear around the bend. "Why don't we come up with some crazy things that will make her want to read better?"

"Like what?"

"You think it up. I'll work on it too." He grinned. "It was a pretty good scare, Crista. I mean, I was really petrified."

Crista wrinkled her lips, then laughed. "All right, it was. But the important thing isn't fun, it's helping Lindy get decent grades and move up to a second-grade reading level in the next month."

As she walked home from Jeff's with Rontu and Tigger on either side of her, she wondered how to get Lindy to "want to," as Jeff had mentioned. It would take a supreme effort, but she knew she could come up with something. If she only had enough time to think it through properly.

·7·
The Treasure

"I can't find it!" Lindy exclaimed as she ran onto the bus after school. "It's lost!"

"What?" Crista asked when Lindy plopped down beside her.

"Your drawing of me! I can't find it anywhere!" Lindy was nearly hysterical.

"Let's look through your backpack," Crista suggested, trying to calm Lindy down. "Maybe it's stuck between some other papers. Jeff," Crista turned around to where he was sitting, "why don't you help us?"

The three of them carefully emptied Lindy's backpack and checked each paper. The portrait wasn't there.

"Well, we can try calling Mrs. Walters when we get to my house. Maybe she found it," Crista said, trying to cheer Lindy up.

But the little girl had begun to cry.

They sat on the bus saying nothing the whole way home. Crista was afraid the special game she had planned for Lindy's tutoring session that afternoon wouldn't go over very well if Lindy was upset.

When they reached the Mayfields', Crista called the school but Mrs. Walters was gone. "I can always do another one, Lindy," Crista offered.

"But I want *that* one!" Lindy burst into tears again. "Everyone thought it was great—except Autumn. She said it was stupid."

It took nearly an hour, but Jeff and Crista finally convinced Lindy not to worry anymore until she knew for sure the portrait was lost.

"Besides," Crista added with a grin, "I had something kind of special planned for today. But if you're not in the mood for a candy bar..."

"I'm okay now." Lindy wiped the last of the tears from her face. The mention of the candy bar had gotten her attention.

"All right," Crista said. "If you want the candy bar, you have to follow the treasure map with the hints along the way."

"What kind of candy bar is it?" Lindy asked.

Immediately, Crista realized she might not have chosen Lindy's favorite. She started to say the name, but then she stopped. "It's my favorite kind."

Lindy's eyes got big. "*Your* favorite?"

"Yup." Crista nodded her head vigorously and folded her arms over her chest. When Jeff gave her a quizzical look, she gave him a quick glare, then turned back to Lindy. The candy bar was her favorite, but she was not allowed to eat candy bars because she was allergic to chocolate. It was one of those horrible "twists of fate" or "God's will," as Crista's mother always said, that you just had to learn to enjoy. As her mother put it, "When life gives you lemons, make lemonade." Crista had learned to enjoy carob chocolate substitute, though she knew it wasn't quite the same. Jeff knew all about her allergy.

"My favorite," Crista said again. "So come on."

Lindy looked lost in thought. Then she began counting on her hands, "There are Hershey Bars, Hershey's with Almonds, Clark Bars, Heath Bars, Fifth Avenues..." She looked up at Crista and grinned. "I have fourteen favorites."

"Well, the one I chose is the top of the heap," Crista said.

"Okay, what do I do?"

Crista laid out the map. Lindy had to follow each step by reading the hints and in the end she'd find the treasure. Each hint had several special characteristics—shapes, colors, and so on. Crista thought it would be a good way to help Lindy learn many words at once and have some fun, too.

The first hint told Lindy to go to the "back to the right side of the house" and "look in the firethorn bush for the second hint." As Jeff and Crista listened, Lindy struggled through the words. When she missed one, both eagerly helped her say it, then waited for her to say she understood.

"Then go," Crista urged. "Last one there's a rotten egg."

Everyone sprinted around the house in their boots and ski parkas. As Jeff stopped to pack a snowball, Lindy peered again at the map and the "hint." She squinted at it, then said, "Which is my right side?"

As if remembering, she held up her hand. "This one!" Then she peered at the house. Crista waited. "But this is the left side." She looked confused.

"That's if you look at it from the back," Crista explained. "But if you look at it from the front, like the hint meant, then this is the right side of the house."

Lindy screwed up her face as if working out this incredible maze of words, then a light dawned. "Oh, I get it." She stared at the bush. "And here's the bush."

"What kind of bush is it?"

Again, Lindy stared at the word. It was a hard one, Crista knew, but it was the only bush she knew the name of around the house. Crista was good with trees, but not with bushes. Except azaleas. She always knew azaleas. One of her favorite places was the azalea festival in Hershey, Pennsylvania that her mom and dad took her to when she was younger.

"Sound it out," Crista encouraged.

Instantly, there was a loud whap as Jeff's snowball struck Crista's back. She wheeled around and yelled, "Jeff, this is serious!"

He ducked his head sheepishly and went back to making another snowball, but this time he threw it at a tree in the backyard. Crista turned back to Lindy. "You have to learn to sound out words. Is there anything there you know? Spell it out and sound it out."

Lindy pursed her lips and narrowed her eyes, trying hard. "F-I-." She looked up. "Fi-re-th."

"No," Crista corrected. "Just the first four letters."

They worked at it for a minute and finally Lindy got it. "Firethorn!" she shouted. "It's a firethorn bush." Then she stopped. "I knew that," she stated matter-of-factly.

Crista and Jeff laughed. They all ran on to the next clue, this time the backyard grill that Mr. Helstrom had built out of stone and concrete. Inside it was a sheet of paper that told them where to go from there. Lindy worked all out and soon they were homing down on the treasure. Crista had placed it under a cinder block she'd found by the road, about a hundred yards up from the Helstroms' house. As they all ran up to the last clue hung on a tree near the cinder block, Lindy sounded out the words. It took her a few seconds, but with some help she discovered the answer.

Immediately, she turned around looking for the block. A second later, she spotted it at the roadside. She ran over and picked it up. Out fell a giant-size Mounds Bar!

Lindy clapped her hands together. "Mounds! Almost my favorite!"

Smiling, Crista and Jeff watched as Lindy opened it, then courteously offered each of them a bite. "Not a whole piece," Lindy said. "Just a bite."

Crista put up her hands. "No, it's all yours, Lindy. And you don't have to eat it now."

Lindy chomped into the dark chocolate and coconut bar and grinned. "No, I'm gonna eat the whole thing *now*!" She stuffed the first of the pieces into her mouth and chewed happily. "This is great. I think Mounds is now my number-one favorite. Behind Hershey's with Almonds. Nothing beats Hershey's with Almonds. But this is pretty good."

As they turned to go, Crista said, "You did really well, too, Lindy. I'm proud of you."

"You are?"

"Me, too," Jeff agreed. "Even if I'm not making twenty bucks a week at this."

Crista gave him a frown, but she said again, "There were some hard words in there, and you hung in without giving up. That's what it takes to learn to read. Just keeping at it. Do that, and you'll get it."

"You really think so?"

"Of course." She draped her arm over Lindy's shoulders and squeezed. "Come on. We'd better get home."

There was a sudden screech of tires ahead. Everyone looked up. Rick's truck that had nearly run them down a week ago careened past the Helstroms' house down toward Jeff, Crista, and Lindy!

"Watch out!" Crista shouted. Jeff grabbed Lindy and they all leaped back off the road into the woods. The truck hurtled by. Again, Cruz was in it and as they went by, Crista spotted a rifle in the gun rack in the rear window behind the seat. She also saw Cruz arguing with Rick, but this time they didn't stop.

As they stood in the woods still shaking, Jeff fumed, "Man, those guys could have run right over us."

"No kidding," Crista said, brushing herself off.

But Lindy didn't say anything. When Crista turned to her, her face was purple. She was trying desperately to breathe.

"She's choking!" Crista screamed.

Jeff swiveled Lindy around, then wrapped his arms around her and bunched his hands in a giant fist under her rib cage. He was just about to pull in when Lindy spit up the chocolate. She choked and coughed. Crista helped her sit down on a rock.

"I couldn't breathe!" Lindy wheezed. "I couldn't breathe!"

Calming her, Crista said, "I think we should go down there now and tell that Rick guy what we think of his driving. Cruz is nice, but he's obviously not getting through." She told Jeff what had happened the last time.

"Who are they?" Jeff asked.

"I don't know," Crista answered. "They just live down in what Lindy calls the falling-down house, right, Lindy?"

Lindy was still breathing hard.

"You all right?" Crista searched her face. Lindy's forehead was damp. She was still scared.

"It was just caught in there," she sniffed.

Jeff gave her bangs a quick caress. "Well, you're okay now."

"First my picture. Now this!" Lindy was on the verge of tears again.

Crista had turned and was staring down the road toward the house. "Maybe we should just forget it," she sighed. "And make sure we run into the woods whenever they go by."

Shaking his head, Jeff pointed out, "No, we should tell them while it's fresh in our minds and their minds. And I oughta sling a stone into their teeth, too."

"You're not slinging any stones, Jeff," Crista said, still staring. "All right, let's go down there. Maybe we can just ask them to be more careful."

"All right," Jeff agreed. "Let's move it."

Stooping and looking into Lindy's eyes, Crista asked, "Do you want us to go now or would you rather go home?"

The little girl shook her head fiercely. "I think we should tell them I choked."

"Right," Jeff said.

They all stood and started down the road. Crista grabbed Lindy's hand. "You walk on the inside. And no more chocolate at the moment."

"Okay." Lindy smiled, but Crista could tell she was still upset.

·8·

A Real Run-Down Place

"I say we just tell them off and leave," Jeff was still angry. "We don't give them a chance to even talk back. Just say it and get out of there."

"Jeff, that's not the way to handle it," Crista answered. "More flies are caught with honey than vinegar, my grandmother says. We can try to be nice to them and at the same time tell them how we feel."

"Then you better do the talking, because I feel like bashing their brains in."

Crista considered going back to the Helstroms' to call the police, but she knew that might only make things worse. And Cruz had been nice about it the previous time. He was the one to approach and maybe act as a go-between. Wasn't that what her mother had always said? Crista could remember a speech her mom had made once when her dad was angry about a situation at work. Her mother had counseled him, "Sit down with them in private and air your feelings without losing control of yourself. Just tell them directly and plainly why it's wrong. They're not going to shoot you over it."

But Cruz and Rick did have a rifle slung across the window in the truck. Maybe calling the police was the best thing to do. No, Crista reasoned, the first step was simply trying to be decent about it. You didn't make peace by making war, unless war was the only way to stop bad people.

They came around the bend and Crista sighted the driveway. The streamlined pickup sat there, black with grit. Tiny spirals of steam rose off the engine. The rifle in the rear window glinted in the sinking sunlight. Neither of the two men were in sight and Crista, Lindy, and Jeff stood in the driveway, not sure what to do.

"Should we just go up and knock?" Lindy said.

Crista looked at Jeff. "Still have that slingshot of yours?"

Grinning, Jeff said, "Right here." He held it up after pulling it out of his coat pocket.

"Then put it in your pocket and don't even think about taking it out!" Crista commanded.

"Aye aye, sir!"

The house before them looked like a rotting stump. Several of the windows in the front were broken out. Shingles from the roof lay all over the yard. And clearly, it didn't keep out water. Bricks from the chimney were sprawled all over. Crista wondered how anyone could live in such a disgusting place.

The front door, though, was nearly intact. Only the two little windows at the top were broken out. The handle was in place, and there was a little gold knocker on the door.

"Let's just go up and knock," Crista suggested.

She started up the icy path. Snow lay in patches in the front yard. Before she reached the first piece of slate on the ground that marked the steppingstones up to the door, there was a squeak and the door opened.

"What's going on here?" It was not Cruz, but the other guy. He didn't look friendly. He strode out into the light. He squinted at the threesome, as if the light were too strong for him. Cruz appeared right behind him.

Crista stepped forward. "We don't want to make trouble. I'd just appreciate it if you'd go a little slower when you drive by us on the road. We take walks a lot and Lindy here is only seven and I'd just appreciate it."

Rick looked her up and down. Cruz stepped forward. "Hey, no sweat. I'm trying to get him to pull up that iron foot of his." He smiled. "We will slow down, won't we, Rick?" He turned and looked into his friend's eyes. Rick only scowled. He had dirty blond hair and deep dark eyes that looked eerie, like one of those monster-type people you see sometimes in old horror movies.

"Look, keep out of our way and it'll all go okay. Got it?" He spoke with a sneer.

Cruz said, "Rick, you don't have to be mean about it." But Rick waved him off. For the first time, Crista noticed Rick had a little dirty brown mustache, almost not visible. His lanky blond hair hung around his head like it hadn't been washed in six months. His flannel shirt had a black stain over the left pocket. He was tall and skinny.

Rick ambled forward a few paces. "Well, miss, I's very sorry ah almost killed you and your chilluns, there. But we on big business. Next time we'll drive on the other side. That okay by you?"

Crista realized he was mocking her. She wasn't sure how to respond. She looked from him to Cruz. She felt Lindy and Jeff behind her, but they weren't saying anything.

"Next time we'll just call the police," Crista replied curtly and turned around, then walked back toward

Jeff and Lindy who were staring with their mouths open, amazed at what was going on. "But I hoped I wouldn't have to do that." She faced Rick again.

"Well, thaz all right, Miss Scarlett," Rick intoned. Crista knew now he was talking like they did in a movie called *Gone with the Wind*, one of her mother's favorites. Crista herself had seen it at least five times. Her father had bought her mother the video for Christmas one year. "But you should know that my uncle is chief of police, and he knows all about us!"

Cruz put his hands on his hips and frowned. He obviously didn't like the way Rick was acting. Crista glared at Rick once more, now really angry about the whole thing. She said to Jeff and Lindy, "Let's go."

Rick slapped his knee with his hand. "Tell the police," he drew the word out, *po-leeeeeeeese* "that Rick sent you. Them and I go way back."

Flexing her jaw with anger, Crista herded Lindy and Jeff back out to the road. When they reached it, the cowboy whooped. "Ho-upppppp! Yee-hah!"

Crista bristled, "I don't understand how people can act like that."

A second later, Cruz finally moved and ran out to them. Rick shouted, "That's right. Go licking their shoes again." But Cruz ignored him.

When he caught up to the threesome, he said, "Look, Rick shouldn't talk to you like that. He's had a bad day."

They all stood there, no one knowing what to say. Rick shouted again, "Go ahead, lick their shoes."

Cruz's face flashed with anger. "He doesn't know the meaning of neighborliness. I'm trying to teach him, but with some dogs you just can't teach them any tricks."

Looking at him, Crista suddenly laughed. Cruz was really trying to make things right and it seemed strange that his friend was so much the opposite. For the second time in a week, he held out his hand. "I know you must think I'm nuts, but Rick can be a decent person most of the time. He just has these moods."

"It's all right." Crista didn't want Cruz to feel too bad. "If you could just get him to drive more carefully."

"I will, I swear I will."

Lindy suddenly held up her Mounds Bar. "Would you like a piece?"

Cruz stooped down in front of her. "No, I don't want to take your candy." He touched Lindy's hair, then stood. "Look, I promise I'll really work on him, okay? And please feel free to stop by when I'm around. Rick is all talk, believe me."

"Thanks." Crista said.

"No. Thank you!" Cruz replied. "And please don't call the police."

"We won't."

He turned and walked back to the house. The three kids headed up the road. No one said much on the way home.

Crista finally broke the silence. "Feel better, Lindy?"

"A little."

"I'll draw you another caricature."

"But I liked *that* one," Lindy sighed.

Crista put her arm around Lindy's shoulders. "I'll make it just like the first one."

"I bet Autumn stold it!" Lindy suddenly said. "I bet she did!" She pulled her hands into tight little fists.

"Lindy!" Crista was shocked by her outburst. "Don't accuse someone when you're not really sure."

The little girl was stubborn. "She did! I know she did! You don't know Autumn like I do."

Crista gave Jeff a worried look. He only raised his eyebrows and shrugged.

This was making things worse. Much worse!

·9·

A Friendly Visit

It didn't take long to discover that the caricature was definitely lost—or "stolen," as Lindy kept insisting. And no matter how many times Crista offered to do another one, Lindy was adamant about finding the "true one." Crista just hoped she wouldn't do anything rash.

The next Thursday, Crista decided to pay a visit to Nadine and Johnny Semms who lived by Moonlight Mountain. Crista took Lindy with her, hoping to take Lindy's mind off the portrait for a while. She promised Mrs. Helmstrom they'd be back in time to do Lindy's reading twice.

Nadine and Crista became friends the previous fall when Crista discovered the Semms living in the old hunting cabin near the dump in the valley between the mountains. Crista wanted to show Lindy a little more about the mountains and she hoped they might even see a deer or two. Rontu and Tigger tagged along behind them as they walked up the trail into the woods. Jeff was not with them. His grandparents were trying to sign him up that afternoon for guitar lessons. Now that he'd seen Mr. Helstrom's guitar, he was set on learning to play lead as soon as he could find a teacher.

Rontu padded behind them and Tigger wove back and forth along the trail. When they came to a special tree Crista pointed it out. She called it "The Love Tree" because it had two lovers' initials carved into it. Crista also showed Lindy some of the different rocks you could find on the trails.

"This is slate," Crista said, picking up a gray flat piece. "It's great for skipping stones on the lake. But not when it's frozen."

Most of the snow had melted now, and only patches appeared here and there. Still, both girls dressed warmly in their ski parkas, hats, and bright red mittens Mrs. Helstrom had knitted for them. Lindy wore her deerskin lined boots, too, and a white parka with an embroidered back that said, "Lindy Helstrom, Number One." Her mother had made it for her for Christmas.

They both sank down to their knees and brushed at the slightly wet leaves on the path. "Oo, what's this?" Lindy asked, holding up a reddish piece of stone that looked like sandpaper.

"Sandstone," Crista replied. "It's hardened sand, anyway I think that's how it's made."

"Hey!" Lindy said, rustling around in the leaves. "Look at this one. I like this one."

The stone was almost pure white. Crista laid it on her mitten and stared at it. "Never seen one like that. Quartz probably. Or maybe an old marshmallow that got hard."

Lindy stared at her. Crista laughed and patted her on the back. "Come on, we've got to get to Nadine's and then back to your house before dark."

Lindy spotted something else. She flipped up a larger piece of something gray and white, like mashed up black-eyed peas. Handing it to Crista, Lindy said, "I know what this is."

"What?"

"Cinder block."

Crista grinned. "You know your stuff! I was wondering if you'd recognize it."

"Yeah, our whole basement is cinder blocks."

They continued on through the woods. Rontu and Tigger sniffed around lazily, not really getting interested in anything. Crista watched out for deer, or dump dogs. The strays that lived at the local dump were all over. Crista felt sorry for them. At one time both Rontu and Tigger had been dump dogs. Crista befriended them, though, and after they made a daring rescue when she was lost in the woods, her dad let her keep them.

"Look out for deer and fox," Crista said.

"And lions?" Lindy asked, her eyes suddenly growing big. When she cracked a smile, though, Crista knew she was kidding.

"Yeah, lions and tigers and bears."

"Oh yeah, like in the *Wizard of Oz*."

"Right."

They came to the place in the trail where they descended down to Nadine's cabin. Crista pointed to a large rock far ahead of them. "Just beyond that is the cabin."

They hurried along. No deer, fox, or bears appeared and Crista was a little disappointed. But since this was her first real outing like this with Lindy, she told herself not to worry about it.

Soon they reached the cabin. Crista knocked at the door and in a moment, tall, blonde-haired Nadine appeared with a baby in her arms. Crista immediately introduced Lindy to Nadine and then peered into the little bundle in Nadine's arms. "And that's Johnny Junior. He has a sister—a twin sister—named Fairlight."

Nadine invited them in. Lindy quickly found the crib in the corner of the room and they all stood over Fairlight talking about how beautiful she was. Lindy remarked, "Much more beautiful than Johnny Junior."

"Oh, you don't like boys, huh?" Nadine said, raising her eyebrows at Crista.

"They're all really dumb," Lindy murmured, not raising her head. She reached down with a finger and Fairlight grabbed it. "She's strong, too."

"How about a soft drink?" Nadine said to Crista.

Soon, both Crista and Lindy were sipping colas and talking about the babies and school and Crista's art. Lindy told Nadine about the picture Crista had done of her and how "Autumn stold it."

"We don't know that for sure, Lindy." Crista frowned.

"Well, I do!" Lindy crossed her arms in a huff.

Nadine showed Lindy the painting Crista had done around Thanksgiving that had been entered in the school contest. In a short time, Lindy brought up the cowboys at the end of her street in the broken-down house.

Nadine motioned to both of them to sit down at the kitchen table. "Tell me about these guys." She was holding Fairlight now, and Crista perched Johnny Junior on her lap. Both babies gurgled and smiled and cooed.

Lindy said, "One's a real crumb ball, that's all."

"Now, Lindy," Crista had a "mother" sound in her voice. She looked at Nadine. "They're just a couple of guys. I guess they think they're cowboys. They wear cowboy hats. One of them, Cruz, is very nice. But the other one, Rick, he's strange."

"I bet they never even rode a horse," Lindy declared, making both Crista and Nadine laugh.

"Have you been to see the Wilkinses?" Nadine asked, obviously thinking of Crista's friends who owned four horses. They lived up the road from Lindy, even though Crista knew Lindy had never ridden one of the horses.

"Next stop," Crista said. "But I had to introduce her to you first."

"Well of course!" Nadine nodded gaily. She threw her beautiful blonde hair over her shoulder and Crista found herself wishing she was as pretty as Nadine. Her dad said she was, and so did Jeff. But Nadine could be a model if she wanted to. Crista was sure of it.

"Are these college guys, you think?" Nadine returned again to the subject of the cowboys.

"I don't think so," Crista said. "Is there a college around here?"

"Sure," Nadine answered. "A small one in Honesdale, I think. And Scranton College, isn't too far away. I think Bloomsburg is close, too."

"I didn't know that," Crista admitted. "But I don't think they're college students."

"Probably just working locally," Nadine mused.

"Probably just messing around till they get married and settle down like you and Johnny." Crista smiled.

Nadine laughed. "Yeah, Johnny was like that, too. Dirty. Smelly. Working on cars all the time."

"I bet they've run over at least six kids by now," Lindy proclaimed with finality. Both Nadine and Crista stared at her, astonished.

"You don't know that, Lindy," Crista exclaimed. "And if they had, they'd be arrested, you can be sure of that."

"The way they drive, they probably forget the minute they run over them."

Nadine looked at Crista incredulously, and Crista laughed. Lindy could be a rip, Crista thought. It made her feel good to introduce her to Nadine.

"You know what?" Crista suddenly asked, looking from Nadine to Lindy.

"What?" both girls replied in unison.

"I bet they could eat up a batch of my chocolate chip cookies in a whiff, and then we'd really be friends."

Nadine wrinkled her brow uncertainly. She glanced at Lindy and then back at Crista, shifting Fairlight on her lap. Johnny Junior was gurgling and a glob of goo slipped down his chin onto his shirt. Nadine reached around with a towel and wiped him off.

"You think you should make them some cookies?" Nadine finally said.

"Make them for me and we can pretend we made the cookies for them," Lindy suggested, her eyebrows raised dramatically.

Nadine and Crista laughed. "No, really," Crista said, "what if I made them some cookies and took them over?"

"Well," Nadine sounded uncertain, "it would show you want to be friends, and it would even be a good way to be good neighbors. You know, the golden rule and all. But..."

"That's it!" Crista exclaimed. "Cruz is definitely decent and maybe Rick'd loosen up if we were really nice to them. I think they're just trying to fix up the house or something. Rick will be hard to break through to, though."

"He's a real bleep," Lindy said.

"Bleep?" Both Crista and Nadine looked at her, smiling.

Lindy sighed, "There are about ten of them in the second grade, too."

Nadine chuckled. "I'm not up on the lingo, but maybe it's worth a try. Most men I know are hungry, that's for sure. I just hope the bad guy doesn't bite your head off." She gave Crista a hard look. "This isn't one of those harebrained ideas of yours, is it?"

"No, I just figured it out," Crista said. "If you stomp up to a person all angry, they act angry in return. But maybe if we were nice, well, maybe they would turn out to be like you and Johnny."

Nadine nodded her head. "Well, you are always talking about the Bible and how we're supposed to treat people right even if they don't treat you the way you want. Didn't you tell me that?"

"Right." Crista remembered the time. Once when Nadine and Johnny had a bad argument, Johnny drove out of the yard squealing the wheels. Crista showed Nadine the place in the Bible where Jesus had said, "However you want others to treat you, so treat them." She had even said, "My mom used to tell me it means treating people right even if they don't treat you right—ever." Nadine had whistled over that one, but after several days of trying it, she was so excited that she told Crista it really worked. Not that it always made Johnny better, but it had helped her feel better about their relationship. Crista realized it was the first time something she shared from the Bible really helped someone.

Still, Nadine didn't look convinced. "Let's think about this, Crista, before you go off half-cocked, all right? Johnny and I are married and have kids. These are just two guys in a deserted cabin. You don't know a thing about them."

"Sure, but even you say all guys drive fast. I've even gone in the truck with Johnny. He goes fast everywhere."

Nadine laughed, "You're right about that." She suddenly turned serious. "Crista, don't get crazy about this now." She touched her hand. "Talk to your dad about it, and also Lindy's parents. And don't go in the house unless there's an adult there. Okay?"

"Of course." Crista couldn't help but feel a little defensive. She knew she sometimes got these crazy ideas, especially when she had a disagreement with someone. She always wanted to make up and be friends. She didn't like the feeling that there were people somewhere who didn't like her.

"It'll work," Crista announced with finality. "I'll make up a batch tonight."

·10·

The Cookie Test

"Are you sure we should be doing this?" Jeff said as he, Crista, Lindy, and Mr. Helstrom walked down the road toward the cowboys' house. Crista had a paper plate full of chocolate chip cookies. Mr. Helstrom wanted to meet the two men, so he took off a couple hours from work to stop by. He and Lindy had already eaten eight of the cookies, and Jeff had six. "Your cookies are too good to waste on these guys, Crista," Jeff added.

"If we don't try to be nice to them, they'll never be nice to us," Crista said with determination. "My grandma always says more flies are caught with honey than vinegar."

"And what's that supposed to mean?" Jeff had wanted to try out some chords on Mr. Helstrom's guitar now that he'd had his first lesson and Mr. Helstrom said he could. He really wasn't enjoying having to tag along to "protect" everyone, although he knew Mr. Helstrom was really there to do that.

"Just think about it," Crista tried to keep the frustration out of her voice. "Lindy thinks it's a good idea."

Lindy nodded. "And if they don't like it, I'll smash 'um!" She threw out one hand and made a quick karate chop. For some unknown reason, Lindy was on a karate kick, something Crista had never seen in her before.

Mr. Helstrom smiled at his daughter's enthusiasm. "I'll just watch the goings on, kids. Make sure these two are on the up and up, all right? Just don't do anything foolish."

"Like what?" Lindy asked.

"Like giving them a karate chop!" Mr. Helstrom answered. Everyone laughed.

When they reached the run-down house, all four of them stopped suddenly. The truck sat in the driveway. They all walked cautiously toward the house. Even Mr. Helstrom looked a bit nervous. Crista wasn't sure whether to go to the side door or the front, but the front seemed wiser at this point. As they all stood on the little stoop by the door, Crista breathed out nervously, then lifted the knocker. As soon as she hit it, the door jarred loose and opened.

"Uh oh," Crista whispered. Jeff stepped back off the stoop and Lindy looked up at Crista with fear. No one appeared or came to the door.

"What should we do?" Lindy asked, leaning slightly inside to look around. The floors were dirty. Boxes lined the walls. Cigarette butts lay here and there, stubbed out and ground into the linoleum.

Mr. Helstrom pulled the door shut. "Knock again."

She struck the knocker and again the door slowly wheeled open. "This is creepy," Crista said.

Jeff started fidgeting nervously. "I think we should just lay the cookies on the floor and get out of here."

"But what if there's a monster in there?" Lindy's eyes grew wide. "Or what if the monster ate the two cowboys?" She looked up at Crista, waiting for a laugh.

She continued, "Or what if the monster is cooking up a big pot with both of them tied up and ready to roast? Shouldn't we go in and kill the monster?"

Crista rolled her eyes at Jeff. "I don't think there's a monster in there, Lindy."

At that moment, there was a loud crash. It sounded like it came from the basement. The muffled sound of someone swearing filled the air.

"They must be downstairs," Mr. Helstrom stepped inside and called. "Anybody home?" He moved inside a little farther. "Hello!" he called again.

Suddenly, music came on, loud and strong on the bass. The whole house seemed to shake. "I don't think they can hear us," he said.

They went all the way to the doorway of the side hall where there was a dining room or maybe a living room. At one time, anyway. Now it was piled with old rusty pieces of metal that looked like they belonged to old cars. A rotting staircase lay directly ahead of them. The steps looked like they wouldn't hold a flea, and there were several holes where someone had clearly broken through.

"Hello!" Mr. Helstrom yelled this time.

No answer.

The kitchen was straight ahead. Mr. Helstrom turned to the children, "I'm going into the kitchen and call down into the basement. Probably a door there. I don't think there's anything to be afraid of." Lindy gripped her father's hand. Jeff's face was white. Crista felt her heart pounding like it would go through her rib cage. Even with Mr. Helstrom, this house was scary.

"What if they beat us up or something?" Jeff said.

"With Mr. Helstrom here?" Crista asked, looking at the big man. He didn't look afraid at all.

"Just calm down everyone. We'll talk to them in a minute." Mr. Helstrom shook his head with exasperation. "They're not going to beat us up."

The kids all tiptoed through the dining room to the kitchen in the back while Mr. Helstrom just walked in. It looked like a normal kitchen, though most of the white porcelain had rust spots and chips out of it. There was a stove, and a monster trash pile with pizza boxes, Kentucky Fried Chicken buckets, and several very clean chicken bones lying on the floor.

"Yuck, it smells." Lindy wrinkled her nose.

Crista spotted a door in the middle, obviously under the stairs that led to the second floor.

"They must be down there." Mr. Helstrom put his ear to the door, listening. He rapped firmly on the door. "Hello?" he called again, not too loud, but loud enough.

Instantly, the whole house became dead silent.

"Who's there?" a voice came from inside.

"Howard Helstrom. I live up the street," Mr. Helstrom replied.

There was the clop of boots on the stairs. Then the door opened slowly. Rick, the tall thin guy, poked his head out. He wasn't wearing the cowboy hat. Up close, he was unshaven, with stubble and the little brown mustache. His face was all smudged up with dirt and grease.

"Hello!" Mr. Helstrom greeted enthusiastically, all the kids crowded behind him.

Rick's eyes slit with anger. "What do you want?"

He was obviously irritated, even with Mr. Helstrom there. "The kids here wanted to give you some cookies." Mr. Helstrom's friendliness didn't waver. "Show they weren't mad."

Crista raised the plate of cookies in her hand till it was right under Rick's nose. "I thought we would make you some cookies. So we could be friends, since we sort of all live around here and everything." After she said it, she felt totally dumb.

Mr. Helstrom just smiled and stepped back, letting Crista do the talking.

A look of surprise, then interest, and finally a squinty slyness crossed Rick's face. He turned around. "Hey, Cruz, come up here." He looked at Crista. "You really made 'em, huh?"

Crista didn't know what to say now. She just nodded. But Lindy jumped in with the words, "They're great. I already had five. Or was it four? I forget, but they have giant chocolate chips and they really taste great."

Cruz joined his friend and pushed open the door so he could see out. Without his hat, his hair looked greasy, and he was also smudged with dirt, but he smiled. He was definitely the friendlier one. The tall guy seemed a little slick, *sneaky* was the word. Crista was so nervous, she thought she would be sick right on the spot, even with Mr. Helstrom behind them. Still, neither of the men seemed angry now. She folded back the aluminum foil. "Here, have one."

"Have two or three," Lindy put in.

"They really are good," Jeff added. Rick and Cruz each picked up a cookie and took a bite.

"Hey." Cruz nodded. "These are better than mama used to make."

"You didn't have no mama," Rick wisecracked.

Cruz looked at Crista and the others. "I know. I was raised by wolves. But I dreamed about having a mama that made cookies like this, and she didn't even make them this good in my dreams."

Mr. Helstrom held out his hand. "I'm Howard Helstrom, Lindy's father. You didn't hear us knocking, so I thought..."

"Don't worry about it." Cruz brushed the incident off with a wave of his hand. "You can bring us cookies anytime." He smiled.

Cruz and Rick finished off their cookies and took another. Cruz pushed the plate toward the children. "Please have one yourselves."

Lindy answered, "We already pigged out. These are for you."

Cruz laughed, but Rick seemed to be watching the four of them as if looking for something suspicious. Crista didn't know what to think of it. Then Cruz said, "Seems like you're doin' all right today. No one runnin' you off the road."

Crista glanced at Rick and he immediately said, "I'm tryin' to slow down. Hard though."

"Well, I'd appreciate it," Mr. Helstrom looked Rick evenly in the eyes. "The kids were really scared the other day."

"We'll definitely slow it down," Cruz smiled, then looked at Rick. "Right, worthy leader?"

Rick shrugged and nodded. "I'll see what I can do. I will. I'll slow down, all the way to 25 maybe. If you're all real good."

Everyone stood around, saying nothing. Cruz broke the silence, "Aren't you wondering what we're doing down in the basement?"

Immediately, Lindy said, "It's not a monster, is it?"

Cruz smiled. "No. Come on, we'll show you." He gave Rick a look, but Rick just watched silently. The kids all turned to Mr. Helstrom, who nodded an okay. Cruz led them to the door. Crista's heart began beating wildly. As if recognizing the fear on her face, Cruz laughed. "Don't worry. We don't eat kids around here."

She felt better and as they started down the stairs, she realized these two guys weren't so bad after all. When they reached the bottom, Cruz pointed. "There she is."

Everyone gasped, even Mr. Helstrom.

· 11 ·

The Project

It was a magnificent speedboat. Long, slim, absolutely incredible! Where had they gotten it? It was blue-bottomed, with a gold and red stripe along the sides and a white top with huge blue stars all over it. The hull was fiberglass, but Rick and Cruz had obviously been painting it to their own special style.

"What's it for?" Crista asked.

As Cruz munched another cookie, Rick gave a little tour. "It's got twin 120-horse engines," he said, and pointed to the two tall Mercury outboards sitting upright on a special wooden contraption to hold them. They were black and silver, huge, sleek machines. Jeff immediately walked over and took a closer look.

"I've never seen engines this big."

"You don't see them much," Cruz nodded. "Them's the biggest, meanest, strongest outboards you can get anymore. Vintage 1980. Old, but they really rip."

"What do you do with them?" Crista asked again, a little miffed no one had answered her original question.

"Racing, what do you think?" Rick snorted. He jerked his head and his long, blond hair threw back out of his eyes. He gave Cruz a hard stare, and when Cruz seemed to think no one was looking, Crista noticed him whisper to Rick. Immediately, Rick grimaced, then turned around. "I'm going back upstairs."

Cruz pretended not to notice as Rick mounted the stairs noisily.

"Where will you race it?" Jeff couldn't take his eyes off the engines. Crista had never heard of big racers like this on the lake, although there might have been some and she just didn't know it.

"Little bit on the lake," Cruz said, running his hands over the slick, black surface. "But eventually, we'll get out on the ocean. Chesapeake Bay, Atlantic City, outer banks in North Carolina, there're lots of places to race."

They all moved over to the boat itself and Cruz leaned against it, smiling and still consuming cookies. Half of the plate was gone now. He got a mischievous look in his eyes. "Guess what we call it."

No one had yet seen a name on it, though Crista thought it might be on the rear end. Then she realized that was usually only on sailboats. On a racing craft like this, the two engines covered over any writing on the back. She didn't see any other name on it.

"The Machine!" Jeff grinned. "How about 'The Machine'?"

Cruz shook his head. "Got to be personal."

"Cruz's Machine," Lindy guessed. She was holding Crista's hand, but Crista could see she wasn't nervous now.

"No." Cruz shook his head. "We call it 'Cruzin' for a Bruizin.' Get it, 'Cruzin',' spelled C-R-U-Z?"

Everyone chuckled. It didn't sound like the best name anyone could choose, but it was their boat, Crista thought. She touched the starry surface of the long bow. The bow took up about half of the boat. In the back were seats for two, with a driving wheel on the right side. It wasn't the kind of boat her dad had, which was primarily for skiing and fishing. This was strictly a speedboat. She figured it must reach up to 60 or 70 miles an hour in a race.

Cruz tapped the top. "It'll be our first summer," he said. "Never raced our own before. So it should be pretty good when we get into it. 'Bout the end of May."

"I'll come cheer you on," Jeff volunteered. He was clearly impressed. Crista thought this was just the kind of thing Jeff would really like. "How far do you go?"

"Different distances," Cruz popped on a blue baseball cap with *Speedo* written on the front. "Ten, fifteen miles. Some up to a hundred or two hundred. We'll just get into the little races at first."

Mr. Helstrom leaned against the stair railing, saying nothing. Crista realized he was observing Cruz, trying to figure out what kind of person he was.

Jeff ran his fingers along the sleek surface of the boat. "Where did you buy it?" he asked.

Lindy broke in, "Can I sit in it?" She looked at her father, and he just smiled.

"Sure." Cruz hoisted her up and set her in the plastic, molded seat in the back. She grabbed the wheel and began turning it. Cruz turned to Jeff, "We bought it from a guy who was upgrading to another model. It's about 12 years old. We've had to do a lot to get it ready for the summer."

"Looks in good shape to me," Jeff said.

"Yeah, after a new paint job, some major hull repair, and overhauling the motors."

"How much did it cost?" Crista asked, running her eyes over the whole length of the boat. She thought it must be thousands of dollars, maybe a hundred-thousand. But she was sure neither Cruz nor Rick had that kind of money.

"Actually, the guy we bought the boat from is Rick's father." Cruz laughed and spit onto the ground. "We're still paying it off. But it's probably worth twenty-thousand now. Or more. With the Mercs and everything else in it."

Jeff gave a low whistle. "Twenty-thousand dollars. Wow! You guys must be rich!"

"Only if we start winning," Cruz admitted.

"Who drives it?" Crista casually asked, looking closely at the enamel on the hull. It was a good paint job. As she looked closer, she realized the stars were decals. Underneath, the paint was solid white.

"Rick does now. We'll have to see how it goes, whether he can hack it. We'd like to find an experienced driver after a while."

"I could do it," Jeff offered right away.

There was a sound behind them as Rick laughed. He had come down the stairs and Crista realized he'd been watching them again. "I think I'll do for now," he said with a half-smile.

"I can!" Lindy proclaimed, still turning the steering wheel fiercely and making a low engine sound. "Rrrrrrr. Rrrrrrrrrrr! Rrrrrrrrrrrrrrrr!"

Grabbing another cookie, Cruz took a big bite. "This is the best lunch I've had in awhile. Don't you think, Rick?"

"I think it's time we got everyone on their way. We have work to do."

Cruz walked over and helped Lindy back out. "So you all live down the road." He set Lindy on the ground beside her dad. "Now I guess we're really neighbors."

Lindy exclaimed, "You should see my dad's guitar!"

Crista noticed Rick listened interestedly as Lindy, then Jeff told them about the Fender Telecaster, the big TV, the stereo, and other equipment. Mr. Helstrom interrupted the animated talk, "I don't think they need to be bored with this now, kids. Time to go."

There was a lengthy pause as everyone stood around looking at the boat like it was a religious worship object or something. Cruz was the first to speak. "So you go to school up there near the dam?"

Crista nodded, "Yeah, all of us. And I'm tutoring Lindy."

"Oh, after school, you mean," Rick broke in.

"Right," Crista answered. "When we get home on the bus."

Everyone had one more cookie as they went up the stairs. Jeff and Cruz talked about the races and when the first one was. Cruz then showed them how the basement was a drive-in basement with a concrete driveway in the back, "That's how we get the boat in and out of the house," he explained. He also told how they planned to fix up the house, after they won some money racing.

At the front door, Cruz invited them to come by whenever they wanted. On the way out, Crista noticed the large garage behind the house. It was enclosed and in much better condition. She wondered what they kept out there, if anything. As they walked up the driveway, she asked, "Do you park your truck in that garage?"

The outside air was chill. Crista shrank down into her collar and pulled her ski hat down over her ears. Cruz turned his baseball cap around backwards like a catcher and lit up a cigarette.

"That's where we live," Cruz said. "But you'll find us mostly down here working on the boat. Come by anytime. And bring cookies!" He glanced hesitantly at Rick. "Okay by you, worthy leader?"

Rick shrugged. "Just so's they don't keep us from doing our work."

"They won't." Cruz smiled again.

Everyone promised they'd come by again. On the way up the road toward Lindy's, Jeff admitted, "Well, you were right. They're decent guys."

"The way to a man's heart is through his stomach," Crista said chirpily.

·12·
Hard Work

On Monday morning, Crista walked out onto the playground at recess. The sixth grade planned to play some kickball. Jeff was one of the captains and after most of the boys were chosen—two kickball washouts, Bennie Klopper and Stan Douma, were always picked last—Jeff took Crista and soon the two teams were ready to start.

It was about the fourth inning when the fight started. Everyone on the field heard it. The second graders had come out for recess and were climbing on the playground equipment. But suddenly there was screaming under the sliding board.

Two teachers ran over. As Crista stood with the other sixth graders on the blacktop diamond where they played, she saw that one of the kids fighting was Lindy. She immediately took off. Jeff was right behind her.

"You're so stupid!" one of the girls was yelling. "You messed up our whole recess."

The other girl, Autumn, pushed Lindy to the ground. "We almost had to stay in because of you!"

"Well, you stold my picture!" Lindy yelled back, picking herself up.

"I did not!" Autumn screamed, grabbing Lindy and shaking her hard.

Crista arrived just in time to see the two teachers pull the girls apart. "Inside!" Mrs. Walters yelled at the three little girls, still struggling.

"She's lying about that picture!" Autumn shrieked.

"She's always making up stuff," the other one was saying. Lindy just hung her head.

Crista caught up to the teachers as they herded the three girls up the side steps off to the principal's office. Breathless, Crista asked, "What happened, Lindy?"

Lindy wouldn't speak. She stared angrily at Autumn. The girl was chunky with a face full of freckles and a mean snarl. For some reason Crista knew she had it in for Lindy. Her little friend was crying now and Crista closed Lindy in her arms.

"No one believes me," Lindy wailed.

Mrs. Walters simply said, "Lindy is convinced Autumn took that picture. It's been war ever since!"

The principal called Mrs. Helstrom at the restaurant and asked her to take Lindy out of school for the day. That afternoon Mrs. Helstrom laid down the law when Crista arrived for the tutoring.

"Your father and I want you to stay out of trouble, Lindy," Mrs. Helstrom began. "Reading and math are the most important things in school. No more fun and games, Crista. I want that full hour every time you come. Half an hour in the reading and half an hour in the math. If your report card comes in with grades like the last time, little miss, I'm going to be very upset."

Mrs. Helstrom was a short, plump lady, with thin dark eyebrows and bright green eyes. She was always nice and Crista really liked her. Even when she tried to be tough like this, she usually seemed a creampuff.

But Crista knew now that with the fight at school, Lindy was in trouble. She suspected some of it was her fault. They'd always done her homework and put in the time, but sometimes she let Lindy take it less seriously than she should have.

Immediately Crista began an intensive program of reading and math with Lindy. They began going over the spelling words and reading books until both their eyes ached. As they worked at it, Lindy finally threw down the book in fury. "I just can't do it, Crista!"

"Yes, you can," Crista insisted. Lindy had missed words like *thunder*, *horses*, *puppy*, and *windy*. Even after the fourth time around, she was not getting them. Lindy was obviously tired, too. But they weren't hard words, and Crista thought there had to be a way to help her get it.

After a few minutes of thinking and listening to Lindy stumble over word after word, Crista said softly, "Maybe we should pray about this, Lindy. What do you think?"

Lindy's eyes lit up. "Oh, my mom and dad always pray with me. I know a good prayer when I go to bed. 'Now I lay me...'"

"Yes, I know that prayer, too. But we need to pray something specific."

"What?"

"First, that you'll start getting this."

"Okay."

"And second, that God will help you work out your problems at school so there are no more fights."

Lindy looked down into her lap. "I don't think that will happen."

"You never know," Crista encouraged. "So, come on, let's pray and ask the Lord to do these things."

They both bowed heads and held hands. Crista prayed briefly, then Lindy said, "Me too, Lord."

They both had a good laugh, then went back to the book. As Lindy read the story about a horse and a boy, Crista thought of Mr. Wilkins's horses. She'd never taken Lindy over there, and she was sure Mr. Wilkins would let Lindy try riding one if she went with her and Jeff.

Mr. and Mrs. Wilkins often let Crista and Jeff ride their horses. Jeff usually rode the big black stallion named Thunder. Crista preferred the gentle Betsarama, a roan mare who was especially friendly to Crista and always whinnied with happiness when Crista stepped into the barn.

"How would you like to ride a horse?" Crista suddenly asked, not listening very well to Lindy's reading.

Lindy looked up with amazement. "A horse?"

"You know, the Wilkinses, down on the farm just when you come in on Rock Road. They might let you ride one, Lukas probably. But only if you get better grades than your last report card. I'll talk to Mr. Wilkins. Then I'll ask your mom and dad. And you have to be able to read this whole book without a mistake."

Shaking her head, Lindy said, "I can't do it." Tears appeared in her eyes. "My brain is always messing up."

"It doesn't when you want to play some trick, or scare me in the attic."

"That's different."

"Oh, it is, is it?"

Lindy hung her head. "I'm just dumb. Like Autumn says."

"You're not dumb, Lindy. No matter what Autumn says. You're actually very..."

"No, Autumn is right! Everyone says it. I mess up everything."

"Lindy, you have to work at it." Crista wondered, though, if Lindy didn't have some disability. She knew about dyslexia, which two kids in her class had and they really struggled with both math and reading. But Mrs. Helstrom said Lindy had been tested and she definitely didn't have that problem.

"Well, if you want to ride the horses, you'll have to work at this. That's all I'm going to say. I'll talk to your parents and see what they say. Will you work for that?"

Lindy nodded hesitantly. "I'll try."

"More than try, Lindy. You have to be determined." Crista looked at her little friend and realized how difficult this was for her. She said, "Put up your fist."

Lindy slowly put it up.

"Say, 'I can with God's help.' Say it."

Lindy shook her head.

"Say it."

"I can with . . ."

"With God's help."

"With God's help."

"And with God's help, I will."

Lindy looked up at her. "You really think this will help?"

"No one ever beats a problem who doesn't decide they can and will beat it, Lindy."

"Okay."

"Let's say it from the beginning."

They did. Then Crista and Lindy punched fists. "All right. Let's get to it."

·13·

A Horse Ride

That night, Crista talked to Mrs. Helstrom about her plan. Mrs. Helstrom agreed reluctantly, "Well, all right, if you think it will work."

"I think it will," Crista said, praying inside that it would.

Within two days, Lindy had the story down. She could read it without a skip. Over the next week, they worked and worked over every detail of Lindy's reading and math till she said she felt like a balloon, so filled up. But when the report card came out, she got a "C+" in reading—a big improvement over the "D" on the last report card. Mrs. Walters had written, "Lindy has shown some real progress. I see her trying now."

Crista even convinced Lindy that until she had some proof, she needed to stop accusing Autumn of taking her picture. Lindy reluctantly agreed, and to everyone's relief things settled down a bit between the two little girls.

Mrs. Helstrom gave them the go-ahead to go horseback riding. Mr. Wilkins was glad to let Lindy try riding, though he said Jeff and Crista would have to walk her till she was ready to try riding alone. He even had a small child's saddle—perfect for Lindy.

The Thursday after report cards came out, Jeff, Crista, and Lindy walked up Rock Road toward the farm. Lindy was excited. "Will I get to gallop? Will we ride like the wind?"

"Not yet," Crista said.

"Oh, sure you can!" Jeff answered.

Crista gave him a hard look, knowing that he probably said that just to annoy her. "A lot of help you are!"

"Just keeping things stirred up," he replied, running ahead down the road.

Lindy bounced along, happy as a blue jay in a mud puddle. She pointed out trees along the road and named them. "Oak! Maple! Pine!" She whirled along, kicked at clumps of snow and picked up pebbles to throw into the woods. Crista hadn't seen her this excited in quite a while.

As they walked along, Rick and Cruz's truck appeared. Immediately, Lindy shouted, "Hey, look who!"

Crista and Lindy waved, and Cruz responded with a sharp wave. Rick didn't wave though. They didn't stop and Jeff turned to watch the truck disappear around the curve.

"Did you see the thing in the back of the truck?" Crista asked.

"What thing?" Jeff replied without enthusiasm.

"Something covered up."

"No, probably something for their boat."

"Yeah." Crista kicked at a pebble, and as it bounced forward, Lindy ran up and gave it a second whack, sending it off into the leaves by the road.

When they reached the Wilkinses' farm and stables, Mr. Wilkins came out in his bib overalls and greeted them all. He had a little grease on his face and a large smudge on the tip of his nose. "Been working on the

Jeep," he said, wiping his hands on an old rag. "Who's going to ride who?"

Crista said, "Jeff'll take Thunder as usual, I guess. Right, Jeff?"

He was walking into the barn and didn't answer.

"I'll take Betsarama anyway," Crista continued, taking off her mittens. "And I thought Lindy could try Lukas. He's the gentlest."

"That's what I thought." Mr. Wilkins wiped his nose and spit on the ground. He led them all toward the stable. "Been setting out a bunch of traps last week for the fox."

"Traps?" Crista said.

"Fox!" Lindy echoed.

"Yeah. A fox is getting into the chickens." Mr. Wilkins had a small chicken coop behind the house so Mrs. Wilkins could have fresh eggs each morning.

"Where are they?" Crista asked.

"Come on. You all should know, so you don't get into them. Jeff!" Mr. Wilkins called toward the barn, "Come here! I need to show you something."

Everyone followed Mr. Wilkins around the back of the house and then the chicken coop. They went a ways into the woods. There, Mr. Wilkins showed them a line of ten traps. "Each one has a little yellow ribbon on the tree nearest it. See?" He pointed to the ribbons. The traps were about five to eight feet apart in a line. Mr. Wilkins knelt down and pointed to a lump of hamburger lying on the ground. It looked gray and disgusting. He wiped away some leaves, though, and there was a trap—gleaming gray steel. Open, it was about ten inches across. Crista knew for sure she wouldn't want to step into one of them.

"So watch out if you're traipsing around in the woods," Mr. Wilkins advised. "I'm going to catch that devil."

They all went back to the barn. There, Crista took Lindy's hand and led her to the back where the horses' stalls were. As they walked along, she told her about the four horses and what each was like. "Thunder looks like *Black Beauty*," Lindy commented. "Did you ever see *Black Beauty*?"

"The movie?" Crista asked.

"Of course, the movie. What else is there?"

"There's the book," she replied, and whispered to Mr. Wilkins, "Lindy's slightly allergic to books."

"I know the type," he said, grinning roundly and heaving a saddle off one of the rails and hauling it over toward the stall where Lukas was. Lukas was a large gray horse with a white mane and a sprig of straight-up white hair between his ears as a forelock. He was old—Mr. Wilkins had told them he was 14—and slow. Neither Crista nor Jeff liked to ride him much because he was so slow and not perky like the other three horses—Thunder, Betsarama, and Dollar. But Lukas was also friendly and if a horse could be cheerful, he always seemed cheerful, usually giving whoever walked into the barn a happy whinny.

Mr. Wilkins explained how to saddle a horse, waiting till they breathed out then cinching up the girth as tight as you could get it. He winked at Lindy, "But since you're a little girl, we won't make you do that yet."

She laughed and whispered to Crista, "I like him. He's cute." Crista hoped Mr. Wilkins didn't hear. He didn't act like he did and just went on with his explanations. Soon Lindy was seated in the saddle, kicking her heels into Lukas's side. The horse didn't move, but simply stood idly in place, chomping some hay despite the bit in his mouth.

Jeff trotted out of the barn ahead of everyone else. Mr. Wilkins called to Crista as she walked Lindy and Lukas out of the barn toward the ring, "Tell Jeff I'd like to see a smile when he's riding Thunder!" He laughed, but Crista only shrugged.

Crista had the reins and directed Lukas through the gate into the ring. She began instructing Lindy how to use the reins, grip the saddle with her knees so she didn't fall off, and use her heels to direct the horse about speeding up. She quickly added, "But you don't need to worry about that yet."

"I'm ready," Lindy said, rocking back and forth. "I can gallop anytime now."

"Not yet. We take this one step at a time."

Crista walked her around, gradually letting Lindy do most of the directing. In about fifteen minutes, Lindy felt comfortable.

"I can do it now," she announced. Mr. Wilkins watched from the side, perched on top of the fence. Jeff had trotted off up the road, but had come back now and began opening the gate.

"Yeah, Jeff, watch me go!" Lindy yelled. She gave Lukas a hard kick and instantly the big gray jolted into a trot. Crista was about to tear after her, but Lindy was holding on well. She bumped along to the end of the ring, then turned and led Lukas back. As Crista watched, she was amazed. Lindy was actually good at this.

"All right!" Crista cheered as Lindy returned to the end. "Ready to go outside?"

"Yes!" Lindy cried. "I want to gallop."

Mr. Wilkins gave Crista a stern look and she said right away, "Don't worry. Nothing faster than a trot."

She went in and saddled up Betsarama while Jeff and Lindy waited. When she returned, Jeff said, "Come on, I want to show you something." He immediately turned Thunder around and gave him a kick, then started up the road back toward the Helstroms' house.

"Slow down, Jeff!" Crista called. "We can't go that fast!"

·14·

What Was
on the Road

Jeff barreled up the road at a canter. Crista grabbed Lindy's reins and held them. "We're not going that fast. Not yet," she told Lindy.

The little girl insisted, "I can do it."

"You don't know what it's like." Crista was firm. "And if you get pitched off in the road, you could break a bone. So forget it for now."

"You just think I'm dumb!"

Crista stared at Lindy, half-angry, half-amazed. "Lindy, I don't think you're dumb at all."

"Yes, you do. Or else you'd let me gallop."

"You have to learn to control the horse and really ride him at the slower paces. You don't know what a gallop is like."

"I do, too!" Lindy was on the verge of tears, and Crista didn't like what Jeff had provoked. He knew they weren't supposed to gallop. Why had he done that?

Crista glanced down the road, but Jeff had disappeared around a corner. She sighed and turned back to Lindy. "I promise you will get to gallop, okay? But it takes awhile. Now just be patient."

"You just think I'm dumb. Like everyone." Lindy's bottom lip pushed out and Crista could see a major disaster was coming. Looking across at Lindy, Crista said evenly, "Look into my eyes, Lindy."

The little girl refused and crossed her arms over her chest. "Lindy, look at me!"

Finally, she raised her head and looked fiercely into Crista's eyes.

"You're not dumb! Did you hear me?"

She nodded her head.

"I never have thought you were dumb in any way. It's just that I fell off Betsarama once and it wasn't fun. I didn't break anything, but it hurt for a whole week. I wanted to go fast like you, but you have to learn it step-by-step. Just like everything else in life."

Lindy bunched up her lips again, then sighed. "Okay." Immediately, she smiled. "I'll go at whatever speed you go."

"Good. Now let's catch up to that bandit."

"Bandit?"

"Jeff, the bandit!" Crista a made mysterious look, and Lindy laughed. "Let's find out what he's all hot about."

They both walked up the road. Betsarama's body swung back and forth under Crista. It made her feel almost sleepy, with the sunlight raking through the trees and the snow melting along the road. A gentle breeze came up, chilling but energizing. As they came around the curve, they saw Jeff off Thunder, stooping by something lying in the road.

When they reached where he was, he looked up. "Come here, take a look at this, Crista. Tell me what you think."

Crista clambered off Betsarama but she told Lindy to stay put. Lindy, for once, obeyed. Holding the reins, she walked over to Jeff. "What is it?"

"Look." He pointed to something smashed in the road. It was brown wood with a number of controls in the front. Bits of glass and shards of the wood lay around it in large splinters.

Stooping down next to him, Crista said, "It looks like a radio or something."

"I think it's an old stereo receiver."

"Where'd it come from?" Crista looked into his eyes. It had to come from someone's car or truck. The dump road connected to this one, and certainly a dump truck could have carried it. But there were only a few places down beyond the Helstroms'. Rick and Cruz were the only ones they knew.

"It's really old," Jeff sifted through the wreckage, stopping at several wires that were tangled up in a broken clump of glass. He paused and looked at Crista. "When they used tubes. Before transistors and computer chips and stuff. Do you think...?" He didn't finish the question. Crista suspected, though, what he was suggesting.

"Why don't we just keep on going down past Rick and Cruz's house?" Crista said. "See if they're around. We could ask them."

"Should we ask them?" Jeff eyes were concerned.

Lindy came up behind them. She had climbed off Lukas without anyone's help. The little girl yelled, "Stick 'em up!" and jammed a finger into Crista's back. Crista jumped. Jeff turned around, smiling, then showed Lindy what they'd found.

"Do you think it belongs to Rick and Cruz?" Lindy asked.

"We don't know," Crista answered right away. She wondered what Rick and Cruz could be doing with something like that. They already had a boom box in the basement. But were they the cabin-wreckers like Jeff was suggesting? That didn't make any sense. Why would Rick and Cruz have allowed them to come into the house and see what they were doing? Why would they even be living around here if that was what they were doing?

Jeff was still combing through the wreckage. "Why would they have an old one like this? I mean, most people don't even use these things any more. They're like antiques. It must have fallen off one of the dump trucks on the way to the dump. That's probably what it was."

"Dump trucks don't usually come down here," Lindy said right away.

"Can we tell which way it fell?" Crista asked, surveying the scene. "Look, it starts out up there with little pieces." She pointed to where the first signs of glass and metal were, about 15 feet up the road back toward the Wilkinses. Looking closely, it appeared to have rolled end over end and finally smacked down where it was now. Later, another car or truck might have run over it.

"So it probably had to fall out of the car or truck or whatever when they were going toward the end of the street," Crista concluded.

"I'd say that," Jeff agreed.

"Sure," Lindy nodded enthusiastically. "Are we like detectives or something?"

Crista chuckled. "No, I don't think so. Just trying to figure out what to do with it." She furrowed her brow with thought. "How many people live down there, Lindy?" Crista finally said.

Lindy screwed up her face. "After Rick and Cruz's I think there are two or three more cabins. I think." She sucked her upper lip and closed her eyes. "Yeah," she opened them, "there's the cabin with the deer head over the door. That's around the bend from Rick and Cruz's on the way to the dump. Then there's another little farm house way down. And then another house at the end, before the turnoff to the dump."

"Who lives there?"

"I don't know." Lindy looked from Jeff's face to Crista's. "Do you think they stold it?"

"Stole it, Lindy."

"Stole."

Crista gazed off down the road toward the bend where Rick and Cruz lived. She was thinking about what to do. But before she could come up with anything, Jeff said, "Let's just gather it up and take it down to them. Maybe it is theirs."

Crista nodded. "We can put it in the saddlebags on Thunder." Holding Thunder's reins, Jeff opened one of the bags and Crista picked up what was left of the receiver. They were able to slip most of the junk into it. When Jeff finally mounted Thunder, Crista warned him, "No more racing, okay? Lindy's not ready to gallop."

"Okay," Jeff answered.

"All right, at a walk," Crista commanded. "Forward, ho!"

Lindy laughed and Jeff said, "Just like in the movies."

All three horses stepped forward at once. In a matter of minutes they passed Lindy's house and headed up the road toward Rick and Cruz's. As they came around the bend, Crista suddenly thought of something. "The radio wasn't there when we walked up, was it, Jeff?"

Jeff answered, "No, I thought I said that."

"So it has to be theirs," Lindy completed their thoughts as she kept pace between Crista and Jeff.

"Are you sure we just didn't notice it?" Crista asked.

"That's possible," Jeff said. "But you know me. I'm usually looking all around. I think I would have noticed it."

"Then what if they say it wasn't theirs?" Crista's voice was quiet. She didn't like what she was thinking. She was so sure they couldn't be the cabin-wreckers! "They just can't be!" she said to herself.

·15·

An Answer

The three children reached Rick and Cruz's in another ten minutes. The truck sat in the driveway, and as usual there was no one about. The green tarp that had covered up whatever had been in the back of truck was folded neatly on the ground. Jeff jumped off and tied Thunder's reins to the back bumper. Then he lifted off the saddlebags.

Crista still hadn't gotten off Betsarama, though Lindy was hanging half on and half off Lukas. Then Lindy slipped to the ground, lost her balance, and keeled over onto her backside. Cringing that Lindy would cry, Crista was amazed when the little girl just hopped up and, like a little baby, said, "Fall down, go boom."

Jeff and Crista laughed. After another moment of hesitation, Crista finally stood next to Jeff looking at the house. "What if they deny it?" she asked again.

"Then we'll know something's up."

Crista shuddered. Her back felt prickly with fear. She didn't like being suspicious of anyone, and especially of people she'd begun to think were friends. They all walked up to the door and knocked. As usual, there was no answer.

"Here we go again," Jeff said. He pushed open the door and called inside, "Rick! Cruz! Anyone!"

A second later, Cruz bounded out from the kitchen. "Oh, we were in the basement," he grinned. "How're you all doing?"

"Fine," Jeff replied.

"Bring any cookies?" Cruz asked Crista.

"Not this time, but we did find something in the road. We thought it might be yours." Crista tried to be enthusiastic, like nothing was wrong. She watched Cruz's eyes to see how he would answer. A moment later, Rick came up behind him. He scowled a little, but when he saw the saddlebag in Jeff's hand, he waited, saying nothing.

"So," Cruz's face clouded only slightly, but he seemed his usual self, "what did you find?"

Jeff opened the saddlebag. "I think it was an old receiver for a stereo."

Cruz's face tightened slightly, but immediately Rick said, "We thought we'd left it. But it must have fallen out of the truck." He stepped forward and took it out of Jeff's hand. "I told you it wasn't battened down." He eyed Cruz, who still looked scared and a little amazed. But Rick, cool as ever, set the main part on the kitchen table. "Where did you find it?"

"Up the road a ways," Crista replied.

"No good, anymore," Rick said. "Completely demolished. Someone must have run over it."

"Yeah, it bounced off the back," Cruz offered suddenly, still looking a little pale. "I mean, after we got home we found the tarp had come loose."

Crista was so relieved, she said, "Did it cost you much?"

"Nothin'," Rick answered. "We found it at the dump, like we do everything else." He raised his eyebrows with a "That's life!" look. "Guess that one's a goner. I thought we could put it on the boat, even though it probably wasn't any good."

Lindy suddenly burst out, "We thought you might have stole it!"

Rick laughed. Cruz said nothing. "You must think we're a real pair of robbers, huh?" Rick smiled at the little girl.

"Yeah, we did!" Lindy admitted. Crista was so embarrassed she felt her face burning. Jeff looked at her and shook his head. "We even thought you might be the cabin-wreckers!"

"Whoa, big time!" Rick really laughed hard. His whole mood had changed and Crista was still a little amazed. Was this the usual sullen Rick? He chortled, "Good thing we're not, huh?" He couldn't stop laughing.

"That's for sure," Crista breathed a sigh of relief, finally beginning to feel relaxed. Why she had ever been suspicious she didn't even know. Sometimes she could be so woozy, she thought. One day she wants to bring cookies, and the next she's ready to call the police. She looked at Cruz and Rick, "We're really sorry. But the cabin-wreckers have us all on edge. They've hit some cabins pretty close to ours."

"Yeah, we keep our eyes peeled," Rick remarked with a chuckle. "We don't want them coming here and wrecking our boat."

"That would really be bad," Jeff agreed. "Can we see it again? Have you made any progress?"

"No, not right now," Cruz said quickly. "We're

working on something heavy and have to get back to it. But drop by anytime. Bring some cookies, okay?"

"I will," Crista promised. "Next time we come."

On the way back up the road, Lindy asked, "Can we at least trot now?"

"Trotting's almost the hardest," Crista said, suddenly feeling very happy and even like laughing now that she knew Rick and Cruz hadn't done anything wrong. If there was one thing she hated, it was having to rat on some friends. Now she didn't have to do anything! I can be such a ditz, she thought to herself.

"Come on," Lindy begged. "Let me trot."

Crista looked at Jeff. "Think we can do it?"

"If she falls off, we pick up the pieces and put them in the saddlebag." He shrugged. "That's all."

Crista chuckled. "It's your behind, Lindy."

"Yay!" She kicked Lukas's sides. But the horse didn't move.

With a loud cry, Crista yelled, "Charge!" All three of them kicked their horses at once. In a second, they were trotting away, all of them bouncing up and down on their steeds. Lindy was howling at the top of her lungs. In a moment, Crista suggested, "Let's sing the 'Battle Hymn of the Republic.'"

"I know that one," Lindy shouted. "Glory, glory hallelujah! Glory, glory..."

"No!" Jeff called. "I've got it. How about 'Camptown Races'?"

"Yeah," Crista answered.

Joining into the song with great enthusiasm, they were soon passing Lindy's house, sounding for all the world like half-crazed New Orleans rowdies on the way to a concert.

"Doo-dah! Doo-dah!"

·16·

One Crazy Ride

Lindy was determined to gallop. Crista thought she had to be the most fearless second-grader she'd ever seen. The next Thursday she talked Crista into another horse ride.

Things started off well enough. Crista and Lindy, without Jeff, clopped off down the road at a brisk trot. Rontu and Tigger were along this time, and kept pace easily on the side of the road. The chill air blew back Lindy's bangs and made her look like a sailor on top of a mast.

"Okay, I'm ready!" Lindy announced. She kicked Lukas in the ribs, but Crista grabbed the reins.

"Lindy, I said no galloping."

"I'm ready!"

"Lindy!"

Crista was off balance. As Lindy jerked the reins away from her, Crista slipped over to the side and plummeted to the ground. The moment she hit, Lukas spooked. He shot forward like a bullet.

"Yay!" Lindy yelled.

Crista jumped up, staring after the little girl. Lindy held on tight. Lukas was really pouring it on. Crista had never seen the old horse rip that fast. For a moment, she smiled. "Well, I guess she has to learn sometime."

But as Lukas neared a curve, Lindy slipped. Crista caught sight of her hanging on sideways and screaming.

"Oh no!" Crista jammed her foot into the stirrup and swung up onto Betsarama as fast as she could. She gave the horse a jab with her heel. "Let's go!" She hit the curve when she spotted Lukas and Lindy still peeling up the street past the Helstroms'. What had gotten into that horse? Somehow, though, Lindy was holding on.

"Don't let her fall, Lord, or get hurt," Crista quickly prayed.

Crista leaned over Betsarama's neck and urged her on. Rontu and Tigger were already bounding ahead after Lindy. If Lukas turned off onto one of the trails into the woods for some reason, or got close to the trees on the side of the road, one of the low branches could knock Lindy off. Crista's heart was pounding even as the horse's hooves echoed in the woods. Lukas's pace was breakneck.

"Please, Lord!" Crista prayed again as Lukas only seemed to go faster. "Jump off, Lindy!" she screamed. "Jump off!"

Lindy didn't seem to hear.

Lukas passed Rick and Cruz's house. Crista shrieked again. "Jump off—before he goes for the trail!"

Lindy was hunched over the saddle. The reins had fallen free, draped over the horse's neck. Lukas was completely out of control. Crista swore she'd never do this again—if they survived.

"Just don't let her go down the trail," she prayed, slitting her eyes as they burned in the chill wind. She had almost reached Rick and Cruz's when Cruz ran out into the front yard.

"What's going on?" he yelled.

Crista didn't slow down. "Lindy . . . the horse . . . out of control!"

There was no hesitation as Cruz dashed to the truck, jumped in, and roared out behind them. Realizing the truck might be better, Crista slowed Betsarama down. "Whoa, girl, whoa!"

Before the horse even stopped, Crista jumped off, turned around, and swung her arms at Cruz's truck. He crunched to a stop on the gravel.

As she jumped in, Crista tried to control her panic. "I think Lukas is headed for the trail. We usually go that way."

With a grinding of gears, Cruz rammed the shifter into first. "Here goes nothin'!" he yelled. He didn't have on a coat, just an undershirt. In the cold air Crista knew he had to be freezing.

"What will we do?" She was terrified Lindy would hit a tree as Lukas careened through the woods.

"We can follow that trail!" Cruz said with determination. "I've driven it a few times just having fun. We might be able to get next to the horse on the straight stretch."

While the road curved to the left after Cruz's house, the trail went straight. It had once been a road, but it was overgrown with small trees and weeds now. Here and there, small and middle-sized stones had rolled down the steep mountainside and settled in the road. Crista knew that any one of them, if Cruz wasn't looking, could tear out the bottom of the truck.

Sure enough, Crista saw Lukas clatter onto the trail a hundred yards ahead of them. Cruz's truck sped down toward it, kicking up stones and dirt behind them. They hit the trail with a bounce that smacked Crista's head into the ceiling.

"Sorry," Cruz said.

"I'm okay."

Crista kept an eye on Lukas's white tail ahead of them. The horse had to run out of gas soon, she thought. If Lindy wasn't knocked off first. The little girl was holding on tighter than a leech. "Hang in there!" Crista murmured as Cruz guided the truck closer behind the horse.

"If I get alongside her, can you grab the reins?" Cruz yelled, glancing at Crista. He looked as terrified as she did.

Gulping, Crista stared ahead. "Like, you mean, lean out the window?"

Nodding, Cruz shouted, "Wrap the seatbelt around your knees, and give me your left hand. I'll hold tight."

They were getting closer. The straightaway loomed ahead. They could do it, if Crista could just get hold of the reins. She wound the seatbelt around her knees, then stuck the metal tongue into the clasp. "Okay." She swallowed hard. "I'm ready."

"Good." Cruz shot out to the left to draw up next to the horse. But suddenly he yelled, "Yo!" and mashed the brakes. The truck swerved and skidded. Cruz hauled the wheel to the right, avoiding a stone. Lukas bolted ahead. Cruz shouted something Crista didn't recognize, then squashed the accelerator again.

"We've got to catch her now or never!" He pointed ahead.

Immediately, Crista saw it. A tree had fallen across the road. The one thing about Lukas was that he had been a jumper—actually a steeplechaser. Crista knew instantly he would jump. And Lindy would never hold on through that.

Crista gritted her teeth.

"Get up on the window ledge," Cruz roared above the wind.

Taking a deep breath, Crista leaned up.

"Give me your hand." The truck was almost alongside Lukas now. Crista could see Lindy's face. Her eyes were squeezed shut and she was holding onto the pommel so hard her hands were white.

"Lindy!" Crista yelled. "Jump!"

The little girl didn't hear.

"Grab the reins!" Cruz shouted. "Pull him in."

The tree was less than a hundred feet ahead. They would reach it in seconds. Cruz's hand clasped Crista's so tight it hurt. She leaned out. The wind blew her hair back and made her eyes tear. The thundering of Lukas's hooves was so loud it seemed to come from every direction. The underside of the horse's body was like a churning mountain stream in spring after a fast hard thaw.

She leaned out. The reins were draped over the horse's neck, free. Out of the corner of her eye, she could see the tree. She had to go for it.

She seemed to be hanging by a thread. Cruz gripped her hand so tight she wanted to scream. She knew she had to get both reins, or Lukas might suddenly turn left and flip over, crushing Lindy.

She flailed out, stretching with all her might. Her ears seemed to fill with a rushing sound. Then her fingers touched leather. The truck was so close now she could smell Lukas's sweat. She reached even further and got the thong on the other side. With a jerk, she pulled the reins down. For the first time, Lukas seemed to notice them.

Cruz hit the brakes as the horse slowed. Crista lost hold. The truck skidded.

Then everything came to a stop.

They were less than ten feet from the tree.

Untangling herself from the seat belt, Crista leaped out and grabbed Lindy's leg. "Are you okay?"

Lindy was still holding on, her eyes squeezed tight. "Lindy!"

Crista touched the little girl's face. She was wet with sweat. Her cap was almost down over her eyes.

"Lindy!"

Slowly, she opened her eyes. "Is it over?"

"It's over," Crista said quietly. Cruz came around the truck and stood next to them still in his undershirt. It was soaked through with sweat.

Crista helped Lindy down. The little girl stood there shivering and shaking. "It was great!" she suddenly proclaimed. "Better than any ride ever!"

"Lindy, you were almost killed."

She shook her head. "I was holding on tight. I told you."

Amazed, Crista looked at Cruz. He shrugged and said, "Just get in the truck. I think I've had enough of a scare for one day."

Crista tied Lukas's reins to the back bumper. His mouth was white with froth, his flanks dripping. They'd have to get him back quick, before he got a real chill. What had gotten into the poor horse?

They drove out slowly, with Lukas trotting behind them. He seemed quite happy with himself about the whole thing. Lindy kept up a chatter the whole time, saying she knew she could gallop, she always knew she could.

Crista just tried to still the shaking that seemed to buck through her body. "Never again," she murmured over and over. "Never again." But deep down, she felt good, even happy. But mostly just relieved.

·17·

Autumn Strikes Again

Gym and recess were outside on Friday. Most of the snow was gone, and the air had taken on a balmy feel. Crista's sixth-grade class had gathered on the two basketball courts at one end to practice layups, foul shots, and dribbling. She saw Mrs. Walters's second grade class come out at 1:15 right after lunch. Immediately, she looked for Lindy, but didn't see her.

It was Crista's turn at the line, so she gave her attention to the foul shot she was supposed to try. She always threw two-handed. The basket missed, and she ran back to the end of the line to await another try. She spent the next few minutes searching for Lindy. Where was she?

When Crista still didn't spot the little girl, she got worried and asked to be excused to use the bathroom. She ran toward the main doors at one end of the building where most of the kids came out for recess. She still hadn't seen Lindy.

On the way up the stairs, she said to Mrs. Walters, "Is Lindy Helstrom out this afternoon?"

"Yes, of course," Mrs. Walters replied in her clipped, terse English. Crista remembered again what a difficult adjustment it had been to the severe, demanding teacher for her four years before.

"Where is she?"

"Out in one of the groups, I'm sure," Mrs. Walters didn't even look up. She was correcting some papers. Normally at recess, most of the second graders did their own thing—jumping rope, hopscotch, football or baseball card flips, or perhaps soccer, kickball, or something else that several of them organized. Crista had been encouraging Lindy to bring some toys with her to school and offer to let others play with them if they'd also play with her.

Crista whisked back out to the blacktop. Autumn and several of her friends were playing jacks on the ground. Most of the boys were bouncing balls or throwing softballs around. Where was Lindy?

Looking over the whole field one more time, Crista finally saw her. She was sitting down with her back up against one of the trash cans. Kids jumped and ran and cavorted around her, but no one was playing with her at all. As usual. Crista walked over toward her. She saw Lindy's pack of Troll cards sitting in her lap. The little girl was going through them, but she didn't appear to be looking at them.

When Crista walked over and stood in front of Lindy at her feet, Lindy didn't even look up.

"Lindy?"

The little girl just stared at the cards. Crista knelt down. "Lindy!"

Finally, Lindy's eyes slowly moved up. She looked tired, almost vacant.

"What's the matter?"

"Nothing."

"Why don't you play with some of the other kids?" Crista knew the answer, but she had hoped Lindy would keep trying.

"Don't want to."

"Lindy, you know that's not true."

Lindy gazed angrily into Crista's eyes, then set her jaw. "Just leave me alone. I'm just doing my cards."

"No you're not."

Lindy sniffed and then pulled out three pieces of paper. She handed them to Crista.

Looking through them quickly, Crista saw it was three very crude caricatures copied from the portrait Crista had done of Lindy. One said, "Lindy the dum-dum." The second, "Who's dumber than Lindy Helstrom? No one!" And the third, "What is stupider than 12 Slobovians? One Helstrom!"

"Did you show these to Mrs. Walters?" Crista asked immediately, starting to feel angry.

"No," Lindy replied. "She won't do anything."

"Well, I will!"

Rising, Crista walked over to Autumn. "You know, you could try to be friendly to Lindy. It's not like she's nasty to you or anything."

"She's an idiot."

Crista gave Autumn a hard look. "Seems to me the real idiots are the ones who are mean to other kids."

"I didn't know you were the teacher here." Autumn looked around at her friends. The kids had stopped their jacks completely and were looking up at Crista. A couple of the girls laughed. Crista looked back at Lindy, but she kept her head down.

Putting her hands on her hips, Crista said, "You could try to include everyone in what you're doing, you know."

Autumn picked up the jacks and the ball. They weren't the old metal type of ages ago, but they were hot green, hot pink, and hot orange colored and made out of plastic. They were bigger, too. "We play with who we want," she said haughtily. She threw the jacks out.

Crista's sneaker slapped down next to Autumn's foot. She stood still, thinking. Looking back momentarily at Lindy, she remembered how when she had been in second grade, some of the kids avoided a boy named Smerrell, a real small wiry kid with thick, porcupine-like hair and a head that was big on top and tiny down to the chin. He often got into fights. Crista didn't want to see that happen to Lindy.

"One of these days, Lindy might happen to have something you want, Autumn." Crista fixed her gaze on the girl. "And why would she ever want to share it with you?"

"She'll never have anything I want!" Autumn huffed, and the other girls laughed.

Crista looked at Lindy, still sitting with her head down. She wondered what the little girl could be thinking. Probably that Crista was embarrassing the tar out of her.

Without saying anymore, she walked back to Lindy. She stooped down and ripped up the three pictures. "We can flip some Troll cards after school today, Lindy," she said.

The little girl suddenly looked up at her. Her eyes were dark, angry, and her jaw set. "Just leave me alone. That's all."

"I'm just trying to help."

"I don't want your help."

Crista gazed at her evenly. Lindy's freckled face looked like doom. "Lindy, it's not that bad. You don't have to take it this way."

Lindy peered down at her cards. Slowly, she got up and they fell off her lap onto the ground. She walked by Autumn and the others with her nose in the air, saying nothing. Crista simply stared. Then she quickly gathered up Lindy's cards and ran after her. As she passed Autumn and the others she overhead Autumn say, "What a dope."

·18·

What to Do

The cabin kept looking better and better. Nadine Semms sat down at the table and offered Crista a fresh buttered English muffin. "Johnny found a toaster at the dump and fixed it," she said. "Would you believe it?"

"What am I going to do, Nadine?" Crista blurted out, not in a mood to talk about toasters. "Lindy is totally depressed. I mean, she won't even talk to me about it anymore. I understand that some kids just don't like each other, but this is way beyond that. Autumn is really destroying her." Crista sighed.

"There is a pecking order, you know."

"A pecking order?"

"Sure," Nadine said, crunching into one of the muffins. She had her beautiful blonde hair pulled back with a leather barrette. In her new pink ruffled blouse, which she decided to model for Crista when she arrived, Nadine looked like a real model, the kind that made the cover of one of those magazines all the women read.

"It's like there are certain kids who are always first," Nadine continued. "And everyone knows who's next and who's next, till you get down to the last one. Chickens do it. That's where the expression comes from.

117

Every chicken in the yard knows where he fits in the order, and if he violates it—er, I mean she. Chickens are she's, roosters are he's, right?" She didn't wait for Crista to answer. "What I mean is, maybe Lindy feels like she's last in line and Autumn's first and since Autumn calls the shots at the top, she feels powerless to do anything about it."

"But she's such a great kid," Crista protested. She fell silent, thoughtfully munching on a muffin. "Where did you learn that about chickens anyway?" she said at last.

"Been reading about them. Thinking about starting a coop."

"That would be neat."

"Yeah, Johnny can't wait for me to cook him chicken 'n brisket."

"Gross."

"Well, we would eat them, you know. We wouldn't raise them just for eggs."

Crista smiled across at her friend. If there was one person she cared about more than her own dad, it was Nadine. But now there was Lindy.

Crista threw back her hair. "All right, but what can I do? I really feel like I should help her. And her parents just seem so caught up in their business. I know they love her and all, but sometimes I think I spend more time with Lindy than they do."

"All right, I get the picture." Nadine took a sip of her tea, then cracked her knuckles. "We've got to get down to work here. What do you think is the most important thing to Lindy right now?"

"Right now? Not being called dumb. And proving she's not dumb to the others."

"And she's learning the reading and math, but she's slow?"

"Right."

Nadine hunched over her tea, twisting her lips and sucking them. It was a bit unladylike, but Crista had seen her like this a hundred times. She always liked the way Nadine was "natural" around her.

"What would make the kids see she's not dumb?"

"I don't know," Crista said. "That's just it. I thought if we could only get her going on the reading, she'd be all right. But it only seems to be getting worse."

"Believe me, the reading isn't the problem."

"Then what is?"

"Look, kids at that age don't notice that stuff that much. It's something else."

"But what could it be?"

"Think back, Crista. Who were the kids in second grade that got slammed around? Even now, who are the kids?"

Taking a long breath and thinking, Crista crossed her legs on the round-backed farm chair. "Well, there are the kids who are weird. Either they're real smart, but always kissing up to the teacher in a way that puts everyone else off, or they're real dumb. But everyone usually feels sorry for the dumb kids unless they're dumb in a way that gets the class in trouble. Like when you're in a group or something. But Lindy isn't like that."

"Yeah." Nadine paused. "Lindy's feisty, right?"

"Yes, but not mean or anything. More playful than anything else." Instantly, Crista remembered something Lindy had told her. She liked to sneak up on people and scare them. In first grade she'd hidden in the closet and made scary noises when just two of the girls were in the classroom alone. The girls had run out screaming. Then Lindy hauled after them, proclaiming it a big joke. Crista briefly wondered if Autumn were one of the girls, but she hadn't remembered Lindy mentioning that. Furthermore, she couldn't imagine Autumn running out shrieking from some noises Lindy Helstrom might manage to make in the closet.

"Did you ever think they might be jealous of her?" Nadine asked.

"Of what?"

"It could be anything. Maybe even you."

"Me?"

"They know you're her friend—the picture and all. You've approached Lindy on the playground, talked to her."

"Kids do that all the time, Nadine. I don't think that's it."

"All right, then. Let's go in a different direction."

"What?" Crista waited, looking into Nadine's perfect gray eyes. Nadine had to have the prettiest eyes Crista had ever seen. Sparkly. The light always glistened in them like she was some country princess. Crista couldn't keep from smiling.

Nadine gave her a curious look. "What?"

"If you came to school with the twins," she began slowly, an idea forming in her head, and walked up to Lindy and said, 'Here they are, your two little cousins,' she'd be the hit of the school."

Nadine laughed. "I can do it."

"No, I can't ask you to do that. And anyway, it would be lying."

Chuckling, Nadine nodded. "It's a good idea, though."

"What?"

"Doing something like that. Putting Lindy on stage for a moment. Letting everyone see she's good at something—besides scaring people to death."

Instantly, Crista snapped her fingers. "Betsarama and Lukas!"

"The Wilkinses' horses?"

"Yes!"

"What about them?"

It was all in Crista's mind in an instant. In two minutes she laid it all out for Nadine. When she was done, Nadine said, "Go for it."

"Do you think they'll let me—us?"

"Why not? The school would probably like it. Who wouldn't? It would break up the day!"

Crista banged her fist into her left palm. "All right, I will talk to Mr. and Mrs. Wilkins tonight."

·19·
The Surprise

"No galloping now, Lindy. None," Crista said as they both mounted Betsarama and Lukas for the long ride down the road to the school. Mr. Wilkins had picked them up in his truck at ten in the morning and taken them back to his farmhouse to get the horses.

"I never thought Mrs. Walters would let us, did you?" Lindy was as excited as Crista had ever seen her. It was the first warm day of March and they didn't even have to wear gloves, though they both wore ski parkas and hats. Both horses blew streams of steam into the air and stamped their hooves on the hard dirt of the farmyard. "I never thought she would let us," she repeated.

"Miracles happen, Lindy," Crista said.

"Yeah, I know."

"Oh, you do, do you?"

"Yup."

"How do you know?"

Lindy's face lit up. "Because I prayed about it."

Crista smiled. "So you're sure this is God's answer?"

"Of course. Who else?"

"Maybe it was just a coincidence."

Staring at Crista with sudden wonder in her eyes, Lindy asked, "Don't you believe in God?"

"Yes, but how do you know God did this? How do you know it just didn't happen?"

"Because," Lindy answered, giving Lukas a little kick. The strong gray horse stepped gingerly forward as if he didn't really want to touch the ground. Crista immediately gave Betsarama a kick.

"That's all you say, 'Because'?"

Lindy stared at her with even greater amazement. "You told me to pray."

"Yes, but how do you know it was God?"

Sticking her jaw out with sudden determination, Lindy stated, "Just because. If that's not good enough, that's tough!"

Crista laughed, smiling at this little test, wondering if Lindy understood she wasn't disbelieving her but just wanting to see if she had a reason for her belief. It was something she'd learned from her mother. Sitting Crista down to pray each night before bed, her mom would always ask about the requests of the weeks and months before. They even wrote them down in a little black-and-white speckled notebook. When an answer had come, her mother wrote it down. Every now and then Crista picked up the book and read through them. And whenever they wrote down an answer, her mom always asked, "So how do you know God did it?" Crista had never come up with an answer. Then one day her mother told her, "You don't know."

Crista had been surprised. "You don't?"

"Of course, you don't know for sure. But you do something else."

"What?"

"You trust that He did answer."

Crista had said, "You trust?"

"Sure. You believe, you trust, you have faith."

Crista hadn't understood it for a long time. Then one day she'd asked her mother, "What does it mean to trust God, Mom?"

Her mother stopped putting the dishes on the table for dinner and looked at Crista. "You are asking a hard question, honey."

"So what does it mean?"

"It means believing the food I'm putting on the table is good for you and it'll nourish you and it won't make you sick."

"I always do that."

"But you can't know absolutely."

Absolutely was a new word Crista had learned.

"It could make you sick," her mom continued. "So you just trust. Nearly everything we do is based on trust."

"What does it mean with God?"

Her mother laughed. "It means believing that He hears you and loves you and will answer your prayers on the basis of His Word. And it means keeping on believing even when things don't look like He hears you and loves you and is answering. Like when I make spinach and tell you it's good and it looks awful."

At the time, Crista had laughed. But she got the point. She was hoping to help Lindy understand as well.

They trotted down the road to the highway, and then down the highway up and down hills. They talked about prayers and horses and playing jokes on kids and how exciting it was to ride a horse right into the school-yard in front of everyone. Right in! Lindy kept up a constant patter of questions and jokes and answers, and when Crista told her about the conversation on trust with her mother, she listened and thought it sounded interesting. "But I still don't like spinach," she crinkled her nose.

Crista just laughed.

They finally trotted onto the school playground and dismounted. Rubbing her hands to warm up, Crista said, "All right, go in and tell Mrs. Walters we're ready."

Two minutes later, Lindy bounded out of the building leading 25 excited second-graders onto the playground. First, Lindy and Crista gave a complete demonstration about how to mount, dismount, guide, and ride the horses. Then they helped each of the kids to climb up and ride. Three of them tried it alone, but Lindy and Crista led the rest around the yard, holding the reins to make sure no one accidentally kicked Lukas and started him galloping all the way home!

When it was over, Mrs. Walters said, "Let's all give Lindy and Crista a big cheer!" Everyone shouted and clamored for them to do it again, and Mrs. Walters promised they would if Mr. Wilkins let them. Then the two girls were off with all the kids watching them trot out of the yard. Crista was sure it had worked the miracle she wanted. Lindy Helstrom would be the talk of the second grade for weeks!

·20·

A Bigger Surprise,
and Worse

The sun shone in fine rails through the trees. The cool air licked at Crista's cheeks. Betsarama's swaying made her feel almost sleepy. Behind her, Lindy suddenly cried, "Let's go fast for a little way!"

Turning around, Crista could see Lindy was still dripping with the excitement of the late morning at school. Lindy had learned much in the last few days, and had even done well in cantering and galloping. A little run wouldn't be bad or dangerous. The shoulder of the road was clear. No snow, just gravel. It was wide enough for a gallop without worrying about traffic.

Crista smiled, "Okay, let's go. But no racing!" Gently nudging Betsarama forward and giving her a quick kick, the horse swiftly moved through trotting, pacing, cantering, and finally a smooth, windy gallop. Lindy was right behind her, shouting and reveling in the breeze.

"It's great!" Crista yelled.

"The best!"

Ahead was a mud puddle. Crista didn't think about it till Betsarama plunged in and through it. Spray flew into the air. Behind her, Lindy cried, "Yiiiiii!"

Crista pulled up and turned around. Lindy and Lukas were covered with mud and water. "Oh no!"

Lindy just laughed. "It's okay. Mom wanted me to take a bath tonight anyway."

"We can't go back to school like that."

"We'll just change when we get to the Wilkinses'."

"I'm sorry, Lindy. I really am."

Lindy just laughed. "It was fun. Next time I get to do it to you!"

"Fat chance of that." Crista wheeled Betsarama around, and again they sped into a gallop for another 50 yards. When they reached the bottom of another hill, they slowed down to a brisk walk. Lindy came up parallel to Crista. She wiped the mud off her jacket.

"Mom'll kill me."

"We can put it all in the wash."

"A ski jacket?"

Looking it over, Crista said, "Well, we'll just have to tell the truth. We had a fight and I pushed you into a mud puddle."

Lindy laughed. "No, I pushed you, you moved out of the way, and I fell in!"

They trotted up the road, laughing and enjoying the sunshine. In a half-hour they turned onto Rock Road toward the Wilkinses' farm. When they reached the barn, Mr. Wilkins' truck was missing.

"What's up?" Crista wondered, dismounting.

"Maybe Mrs. Wilkins is here."

They led the horses inside and opened the stall gates. Then Crista took out the bits and uncinched the saddles. She hung the bits up and set the saddles on their respective sawhorses. She turned to Lindy, "We'll have to brush them down. But I'll run in and find out where Mr. Wilkins is."

Lindy took the coarse brush and began smoothing Lukas's chest, face, and neck. Crista walked out of the barn to the back door. Mrs. Wilkins answered when she knocked.

"Oh, Rollie had to go into town. He'll be back in a few minutes though. Would you like some hot chocolate?"

Shaking her head, Crista said, "I sprayed Lindy with mud water. She needs to change. We'll just walk down to the Helstroms' and change. Then we'll be back. Maybe Mr. Wilkins will have returned by then."

"Sure, I'll tell him." Mrs. Wilkins smiled. She was a short, plump lady with a wide smile and a happy air. Crista especially liked her German chocolate cakes. They were even better than the ones the Helstroms had at the restaurant.

Crista returned to the barn and found Lindy finishing up Lukas. The horse looked fresh and cheerful, though a little tired. Crista nuzzled his nose and gave him a kiss. "Have a good time today, Lukas, old boy?" The horse whinnied and Lindy patted his flank.

"Lukas is my favorite, but someday I want to ride Thunder." Lindy gave Crista a grin.

"You'll get to. Let's finish up Betsarama."

"She's not as dirty."

"I know, but we need to get her ankles—they're caked. And we should just make her feel better after we took such a long ride." The two of them worked on Betsarama for the next few minutes. When they were finished, Crista clapped her hands together, knocking off the dust, and said, "All right, let's get you cleaned up at home and by then Mr. Wilkins will be back."

"Race?" Lindy said, already darting toward the barn door past Thunder in the next stall.

"Lindy!" Crista wheezed as she started after her. "Stop!"

But Lindy was already out of the yard toward the road by the time Crista reached the door. She leaned forward and pushed herself into a sprint, finally catching Lindy about 20 yards later. She grabbed the little girl at the shoulder and slowed her down. "Let's walk," Crista panted. "I'm tired."

Lindy smiled. "Just wanted to see if I could beat you."

"All right, you did. Is that fair enough?"

"Yup!" Lindy gave her an exultant grin. As they walked, she talked about the "show and tell" at the school. "Did you see Autumn's face when I cantered around the yard? Like she was about to explode."

"But she let you lead her around."

"Yeah. That was good. I bet she's jealous."

"Don't push your luck, little girl."

Grinning, in the sunlight Lindy's face looked like a little leprechaun with freckles. "I'm number one now."

"Don't take it too much to heart," Crista chuckled. "It always passes."

"But it feels good anyway."

"Yeah, I know." Crista thought back to times in her life when she'd been "number one." Last fall, she'd won a special prize for her artwork and that had probably been the top. But then Jeff and she had been in a clown competition at the Winter Festival on Ice just a month-and-a-half ago. And that had been a lot of fun. They'd won a prize there, too. It made her happy to know that for once Lindy felt that way. There had been so much stress in school the last couple of months for her.

They turned up the driveway to Lindy's house and mounted the porch stairs. Lindy said, "I hope the heater's working."

"The heater?"

"Yeah, Daddy had all those silver things in the basement . . ." She squinted at Crista. "What are they called? You know, the silver-gray metal things that make the air go to different places."

"Ducts."

"Right. Daddy had them apart last night. Something with the heater. I don't know. But the house was really cold last night and this morning. He was supposed to finish it, but he probably had to go to the restaurant. Maybe we should just stay home this afternoon and fix it for him."

"Cut school, you mean?"

"Yeah!" Her eyes lit up.

Crista opened the door with the secret key. "I don't think so, Miss Tish."

"Miss Tish! What's that supposed to mean?"

"Something my mom always called me when I was being persnickety."

"Persnickety! I'm not that." Lindy looked at her wonderingly. "What's it mean?"

"Forget it!" Crista laughed. "Let's get you changed."

They stepped into the family room on the way to Lindy's bedroom. Suddenly, Lindy gasped. "The guitar and amplifier—they're gone!"

Crista swallowed. "And the stereo stuff!" They both stared. Crista stopped Lindy and they both sank down. "We have to find out what's happening."

After looking around, they heard voices in the back at the kitchen door. Crista gasped. "It's Rick and Cruz."

"Oh, no!" Lindy whispered.

Crista grabbed her hand. "We can't make it back out," she said. The men were coming around through the living room by the front door. "Let's go to your mom and dad's room and call the police."

They both tiptoed quickly through to the hall beyond the family room. The carpet kept them quiet. The voices drew nearer. Just as they reached the bedroom door, they heard the two men walk into the family room.

"What else?" Crista heard Rick say.

Cruz answered, "I still don't think we should be doing this, Rick. They were our friends."

Crista slowly closed the bedroom door. She didn't hear Rick's reply. So they were the cabin-wreckers!

Lindy had the phone.

"Dial 9-1-1," Crista directed.

"I know," Lindy answered, but her hands were shaking and she couldn't dial.

"Here, let me have the phone," Crista held out her hands.

Lindy turned toward Crista to give her the phone, but it slipped and clattered to the floor with a clang! Lindy and Crista froze. Had Rick and Cruz heard them?

"Hey," Rick shouted. "There's someone here!"

Lindy ran toward the door and started to lock it, but it was too late. Rick shoved it open and was staring at Lindy and Crista. Cruz was right behind him.

Crista screamed. Cruz grabbed Lindy. Rick saw the phone on the ground and in one swift motion put it up to his ear. Then he ripped the cord out of the wall.

"We are into it now," Rick said grimly to Cruz as he grabbed Crista by the arm.

·21·

Danger!

Lindy kicked and shouted, "I'll get you for this! I'll get you!"

Rick just scowled. "We thought we had pretty good cover with you all coming around and not finding anything. But you're supposed to be at school."

"So that was it," Crista said angrily. "You thought you could rob the Helstroms' while we were at school and everyone would think it was the cabin-wreckers and no one would suspect you."

Rick gave her a thumbs up. "Smart kid, isn't she, Cruz?"

"Shut up!" Cruz's face looked dark, angry, scared. The only other time Crista had seen Cruz upset was when they'd gone to the run-down house to tell them off about speeding up Rock Road.

Rick rubbed his chin. "We've got a real problem, Cruz."

"Yeah, I know." He looked worriedly at his friend and then back at Crista. "What are we gonna do?"

"I don't know. We can't just leave them here."

"The police will come." Crista set her jaw. She tried to see whether Rick and Cruz had any weapons with them, but she couldn't tell.

"Oh, no. There was only a dial tone on that phone," Rick sneered. "No police this time." He wrenched Crista's arm behind her back. It felt like it would break, but then he eased up.

Looking around, Rick suddenly threw Crista on the bed. "The doors lock on the outside," Rick said, walking to the door and looking at it. The key was still in it on the inside. "We shut it and lock it. That'll hold them." He walked out of the room, checking the doors.

Cruz suddenly turned to Crista, "I didn't mean for you to know this."

"I guess it's too late for that," Crista replied.

Cruz's face was a mixture of pain and fear. "We're not going to hurt you, I swear. But please don't do anything right now, okay?"

"I'm not going to move." Crista folded her arms, feeling betrayed. Rick and Cruz had been lying to them all along.

Cruz held Lindy tightly and the little girl struggled. But Cruz was far bigger than she was. "Crista," he whispered, "Rick won't put up with any nonsense. Please understand that. I'm not that way, but Rick is."

"I know," she said, her voice quavering. "And I thought you were decent people." There was a banging sound in the other room. Then Rick appeared with a hammer and nails in his hands. He dragged Lindy out the door and into her room.

Crista started toward the door, but Cruz shook his head menacingly. "I would just keep still, Crista. You don't know what Rick is like. I'm sure he won't hurt Lindy."

"How could you do this, Cruz? I thought we were friends."

Cruz coughed and couldn't look her in the eyes. "Rick said we needed to put up a good front. If it wasn't for that boat, we wouldn't have to do this. But we have to win this year. It can't be stopped. And we can't make enough at real work. Rick just thinks it's much easier to rob houses and sell the take to some people we know. I would work, but it would take too long. I didn't want you to know about this. Rick never really thought of hitting this place until Lindy and Jeff talked about it so much. This is one of the best ones we've found so far. Most of the others just had junk."

"So that's why you wrecked them?"

"No, that was Rick. You know, he's so mad all the time."

Crista just stared at Cruz. She had brought them cookies, made friends. Cruz had even rescued Lindy—just last week. There had to be something good inside of him. "So why did you help me last week with Lindy?"

Cruz's face flinched. "I couldn't let her get hurt. Afterwards, Rick said it was really good for our cover—not that I planned it that way. But after that, we thought we could hit this place and never be caught. Until you happened by. I didn't want to hurt any of you."

"And this isn't hurting us?"

Cruz's eyes met hers. "I didn't want this to happen. I really didn't."

Rick came striding back into the bedroom. When Crista caught his eye, she shivered inside. His eyes looked even darker, deep in their sockets like two dead coals. She mustered up her courage, "And what are you going to do, Rick? We know who you are and where you live."

"That does present a problem," Rick gave Cruz a sly look. "A very big problem."

He said to Cruz, "The kid's bedroom is all nailed up. I nailed the windows and the door shut after I locked it. I'll do the same here. They won't be able to get out. We'll leave one here and the other one there until we figure out what to do." As Cruz watched Crista, Rick nailed the windows shut. Crista sat on the bed trying to think of something to do. Then, with determination, she jumped up and banged on the wall before Cruz could stop her. "Lindy! Lindy! Are you all right?"

Lindy's voice fluttered through the walls. She was obviously crying. "Yes!"

Turning to Rick with fire in her eyes, Crista said, "You're a mean, rotten..."

Rick just laughed and pushed her back onto the bed. "Just sit tight, Crista. Better be quiet, and don't break any windows, or we'll break you. Got it?"

Crista sat down on the bed. Rick closed the door. She heard him turn the key on the outside and it clicked. Then he banged in a nail. When his footsteps faded in the hallway, Crista ran to the door and turned the handle. It was locked. Tight. And the nail would hold if the lock didn't.

Tears burned into Crista's eyes. What were they going to do? How could they do this—especially Cruz?

· 22 ·

Even Bigger Trouble

Crista stood at the door and listened. Through the wall to her right she heard a faint tapping. She tapped in response. It was Lindy. Crista had heard of something called Morse Code, but she didn't know it. She listened, and whispered, "Lindy! Lindy!"

The little girl answered, "I hear you. What are they going to do to us?"

"I don't know." Since she and Lindy could identify the robbers, Rick and Cruz would have to disappear. But would they leave the boat? And couldn't they be found fairly easily through their license plates?

The moment Crista thought of that she ran to the back window. Yes, there was the truck in the back—and the license plate number. She quickly found a pen and piece of paper on the dresser and wrote down the number.

Thinking some more, she thought of writing a note. But then a chill thought hit her. If Rick and Cruz couldn't leave the area because of the boat, they'd have to silence Lindy and her completely!

The thought was so scary, Crista cringed. They had to get out. But how? She looked at the window. It was a typical older type of window, with eight panes all in a lattice of wood. It would be impossible to break without making a lot of noise. And Lindy would still be caught. She couldn't risk that.

She looked down at the paper. "Okay, okay, think." Trying to stay calm, she prayed, "Lord, please show me what to do."

For a second she waited, then wrote on the piece of paper what she knew. Rick's and Cruz's names. The license plate number. What they'd done. She set the paper—folded—on the dresser. Considering again, she took another piece and wrote the license plate on it, then stuffed it into her pocket.

"Now what to do?" she said out loud.

She listened intently, trying to think of what could happen next. But she couldn't think past the idea that Rick and Cruz might do something worse than leave them in the rooms. In the silence, she heard the sound of an engine. She looked out the window and saw a truck pull into the yard. It was Mr. Wilkins!

Crista moved fast. She had to warn him. He could get the police!

Picking up a chair, she was about to smash through the window. But out of the corner of her eye, she saw Rick in the backyard. And this time he had his rifle trained on Mr. Wilkins's chest. The older man put up his hands. His mouth moved, but Crista could not hear what he said.

"Oh, Lord," she moaned. "What are we going to do?"

Seeing Mr. Wilkins being taken inside, Crista listened again at the door. She heard Cruz and Rick shouting and swearing. She couldn't make out what they were saying, till she heard Cruz walk back into the hallway. There was a knock at the door. "Crista?"

She didn't answer. There was another knock. "Please answer, Crista, or Rick will hurt your old man friend here."

There was a silence, then she heard Mr. Wilkins's voice. "You don't have to break it!"

Crista yelled, "I'm here! I'm here!"

"All right."

Crista backed up. The key didn't turn, though, and the nail wasn't removed. They were simply making sure she was still there.

She listened and heard Rick saying, "We tie up the old guy inside. You go out and get the can of gasoline in the back of the truck."

"What are you gonna do, Rick?"

"Just shut up and do what I tell you."

Fright churning through her, Crista froze at the door. She then darted around the room, looking for something, anything. She had to get out. Fast.

She hurried over to the window and peered at the nail holding the latch in place. She knew she couldn't remove it. As she stood there, she looked down at her feet. She was standing on the grate for the heating ducts. As she looked at it, she knelt down and tried to figure out how to open it.

A moment later, she heard a noise. Not from the door this time, or the hallway. From inside the duct!

·23·

One Chance

Crista listened. It was a scratchy noise, with sudden bell-like "iiiips" that she remembered hearing ducts make when you pushed them in or out. She bent closer to the duct and listened. Another sound. Huffing. Like someone breathing.

Someone was in the duct!

Instantly, Crista remembered Lindy's terrific hiding place. So this was it! She whispered into the grate, "Lindy! Is that you?"

"Yes!" Lindy's voice echoed loudly down the long, enclosed space.

Working to pull off the cover, Crista found herself tumbling backwards when it suddenly released. She bent down to look inside. She could see Lindy's head as she grunted and breathed, pulling herself along through the space. Lindy reached up and grabbed one of the cracks where the ducts were joined, and pulled herself along.

"It's hard going!" Lindy wheezed. "But not too bad."

Ten seconds later, Lindy's face appeared in the hole. She grabbed the edge and pulled herself out. A moment later, she stood in the room.

"Did you hear them?" Crista asked. "They're going to bring in gasoline."

"And they got Mr. Wilkins."

"What can we do?"

Lindy screwed up her face. "There's one thing."

"What?"

"Do you think you can fit in the ducts?"

Crista looked down at her legs and waist, then stooped and peered into the duct. "It's wide and pretty deep. You're not that tight in, are you?"

"No, it's easy for me."

Crista felt slightly elated. "That's where you hide when you play hide-and-seek, right?"

"Not telling!" Lindy grinned.

"All right," Crista returned the grin. "But can we get out?"

"I think so," Lindy answered. "When I passed the place where it goes down to the heater, I saw light. My dad hasn't connected the ducts yet, so we can get out in the basement."

"Let's go," Crista was anxious to get their plan underway. "You first. I'll follow."

"You have to go on your back," Lindy said, already beginning to crawl in, showing Crista how she jack-knifed in feet first.

When she had disappeared inside, Crista went to the door one last time and listened. She thought she heard something being hauled out of the family room. Probably the big television. Naturally, Rick and Cruz weren't going to stop stealing everything, she thought angrily. How could people be like that, especially when you trusted them and thought they were even decent? It only made her angrier.

She hurried back to the duct and slid in feet first. Listening as she pushed herself along, she heard Lindy whisper, "Get up on your side to go down to the heater."

Crista shoved herself along. The duct was high enough that she didn't feel tight at all. She swallowed hard and prayed, "Please get us out of this with no one hurt, Lord. Please."

Reaching the L-joint of the duct work, Crista shifted onto her side and slid her legs down into it. Craning her neck, she pulled back and could see the light at the end, still blocked by Lindy.

"Almost there," Lindy called quietly, her voice echoing in the chamber.

Crista slid along as fast as she could. She heard Lindy gasp, then the metal spring back. Lindy was out! A moment later, Crista felt her legs hit open space. She pushed herself slowly into the opening. When her legs were out, she rolled around onto her stomach. Her legs hung down and she pushed herself out, grabbing the edge at the last second and jumping down.

"Whew!"

"Yeah, me too," Lindy agreed. The basement was dark, but light filtered in through a number of small windows along the edges. "What do we do now?"

"Your mom probably locked the door upstairs, right?"

Lindy nodded. "She's real careful about that. I think she thinks there's a monster down here. And the main doors are locked too. Dad has a key upstairs on the key rack."

Walking over to the doors in the back, Crista looked at the padlock on the inside. The whole place was closed off. There was a large workbench along a back wall, all sorts of furniture covered up in blankets, and two boats and an old jalopy in a corner. Crista stopped a moment at Herbert's cage and Lindy walked over immediately, taking the little guinea pig out. "I can't leave Herbert here," she said.

"Why don't you leave him in there until we figure a way out, okay? I'll need your help."

"Okay." Lindy carefully set Herbert down.

Looking up the stairs, Crista peered up to the sliver of light at the bottom of the door. She thought through several things to do, then walked over to the work-bench. There were screwdrivers, pliers, all kinds of electric tools, a hatchet, and an axe. Next she saw a chainsaw, a boat motor, and a big orange radio with a large round dial. Crista almost laughed. Just what they needed. A radio! There was also a bathroom with a shower in the far corner.

It suddenly occurred to her that Rick or Cruz would probably come down here, knowing there might be something worth stealing. She whipped around. "All right, let's pray that they come down here."

"Pray?" Lindy looked at her aghast.

"Only Rick or Cruz can open the door so we can get out. Of course, we could chop down the door, if anything else happens. But we still have to get Mr. Wilkins, or help, whichever comes first." Crista looked around. "Do you have some fishing line, something black or colorless, that can't be seen?"

"Yeah." Lindy ran over to one of the walls where Crista saw a whole column of fishing rods and gear. They opened up a tackle box. There was a yellow-handled knife in it that Crista took out, and a spool of black line.

"Okay," Crista said. "Let's tie the line across the two beams by the stairs, right across the stairs. If one of them comes down, he'll trip. Then we can run out."

"Yeah!" Lindy cheered quietly.

They stretched the line across the stairs, about a foot up. Crista doubled it and tripled it before she tied it. "Go up and listen at the door, Lindy. See if you hear anything."

Lindy crept up the stairs, while Crista got the hatchet from the work bench. She opened the knife and laid it on the floor where she intended to watch. As she worked, she prayed, hoping that this was one prayer God would answer quickly. Like in the next minute.

By the duct work, she saw several rolls of thick, silver-colored tape. She'd seen movies where thugs tied people up in tape like that. Picking it up, she thought it might be a good way to tie someone up quick.

Suddenly, Lindy was at her side. "They're arguing upstairs about the gasoline," she said. "But I don't think they're going to burn the house down."

"Thank You, Lord," Crista whispered.

"But Rick told him they have to do something quick."

Swallowing with worry, Crista tried to stay calm. "Okay, we have to get out. So here's what we need to do." She explained about the duct tape, the hatchet, and the knife. Then she walked over to the workbench. "Maybe if we turn on the radio real loud, they'll check it out. Pray and hope that it'll only be one of them. Preferably Rick. He's definitely running this thing. I don't think Cruz even wants to be involved."

"How can they do this?" Lindy exclaimed, then covered her mouth and glanced up the stairs. Crista put her finger to her lips.

"Shhhhhh."

With big eyes, Lindy waited. "Get over there behind the boat," Crista whispered. Lindy scurried over behind it. Finding the radio switch, Crista flipped it.

Nothing happened.

"It has to warm up," Lindy called in a low voice. Crista waited. Ten seconds later, the little box crackled and then the rollicking sound of a song began. It was not loud enough yet.

Her heart nearly banging through her chest, Crista turned the volume all the way up. Immediately, the whole basement seemed to fill with sound. She jumped back, then ran around to where Lindy was. As they stood there in the dark, she prayed, "Please, God, please make just one come down."

Lindy said, "This is more exciting than today at school."

Crista looked at Lindy amazed. "If we get out of this alive, I never want it to happen in my life again."

"Me, too," Lindy agreed. "But one time is nice."

Sighing with amazement, Crista turned her eyes to the stairs. Nothing was happening. What were they doing?

Then there was shouting upstairs. The door opened. Rick's voice could be heard in the stairwell. "I'll check it out. You watch the old man. And get the silverware out."

Her heart in her mouth, Crista watched as Rick stepped cautiously down the stairs. She stopped breathing. Lindy's hand was on her arm, squeezing. Rick bent down to look over the stairs. He was two stairs from the fishline.

Instantly, Crista realized, if he went too slow, he might feel it and stop. Then they were done for!

A second later, she knew what she had to do. She murmured to Lindy, "Don't move until I say."

Crista bolted out from behind the boat. "Help! Police! Police!"

·24·

A Piece of Luck?

Rick shouted at Crista as she ran around in front of the stairs. Her heart seemed to pop into her throat. But the tall, slim man stepped down toward her. The moment he snagged the fishline, he fell face forward. Crista turned just in time to see him smash into the workbench. He tumbled into a heap.

Crista stared. Lindy stood wide-eyed behind the boat. Finally, she said, "Is he dead?"

Crista tiptoed over to the still form. She nudged his leg, but he didn't move. Didn't even groan. She looked up the stairs. The radio was still blaring. Cruz wouldn't have heard anything above that noise.

She knelt down and felt Rick's neck. The tiny bump-bump of his pulse was strong under her fingertips. She turned to Lindy, "Let's drag him into the bathroom. Get the duct tape."

Picking up the tape, Lindy watched as Crista took Rick's legs and turned him around. She rolled him over. His eyes were closed. His forehead and nose were bloody. She began dragging him toward the bathroom. Lindy joined her, taking one leg. Rick wasn't that heavy. Once they got him inside, Lindy took one roll of the tape and wrapped it around his feet. Crista rolled him over face down, pulled his arms behind his back, and wrapped them with the other roll. Then she wrapped more tape around his mouth, careful to let him breathe through his nose.

After wrapping his arms and feet, Crista dragged him into the small shower at the end of the room. She closed the curtains.

"All right," she whispered. "Now we wait for Cruz. I'll turn off the radio. That may bring him down. When he gets here, he'll look around. We have to be ready to go up the stairs the moment he goes into the bathroom. Okay?"

Lindy swallowed. "Okay."

"Get Herbert."

"Okay."

Lindy took the guinea pig back out of his cage and hid over behind the boat. Crista clicked off the radio. It crackled and hissed. The whole room was instantly silent. She ran back over to where Lindy was, then stopped. "Let's go over behind the heater," she said. "We can get away from there easier."

About to move, she remembered the yellow fishing knife and spotted it on the concrete near the side of the stairs. She picked it up, closed it, and slid it into her jeans pocket. She placed the hatchet inside one of the boats.

Then they both crept around behind the boats and furniture to the heater on the far side. There was a space in the back. She and Lindy slipped into a crevice near the workbench. She could see the stairs if she bent around the edge of the heater. Lindy had Herbert in her hand. She whispered, "Do you think he'll come?"

"Sooner or later. Just..."

Lindy cut her off. "I know. Pray."

Crista grinned. "Right."

They waited in the dark. Soon, they heard Cruz's voice above them. "Rick! Hey, Rick! What's going on down there?"

There was no answer. Crista heard Cruz mumble something, then she saw his shadow on the stairs from the light at the top. "Rick! Hey, what's going on?"

Crista suddenly made a muffled sound. "Mm-mmmm-mmm."

Cruz walked cautiously down stairs. When he saw the broken string, he stooped down to look. "Rick! Where are you?"

Waiting, Crista pressed Lindy's hand. Lindy caressed the little guinea pig to keep him from chirping.

"Rick, are you okay?" Cruz stepped all the way down to the floor, looking around. He had a knife in his right hand. "What's going on here?"

Keeping out of sight, Crista listened for the sound of Cruz coming closer or moving away. His boots crunched slowly on the concrete.

They both waited, their hearts banging away in their chests. Cruz was walking slowly around the boats. Crista prayed madly that something would happen to keep him away from them.

Then something did. There was a loud boom from the bathroom, like the sound of sheet metal being hit with something blunt. Crista thought it had to be Rick kicking the side of the shower with his boot. Cruz turned around. "Rick?"

There was another sharp metallic boom.

"Ready," Crista whispered to Lindy. She nodded in reply.

Cruz came around into her view. He listened at the door of the bathroom. "Rick?"

One more sharp clang.

Cruz kicked open the door and stepped inside. With one more clang still resounding in the air, he bounded to the shower.

Crista led Lindy around the back of the heater behind the stairs till they came up on the other side. They would be out of sight until they stepped around. But Crista had a better idea. She lifted Lindy up with Herbert in her hand. Lindy ducked under the rail and stood on the stairs halfway up. "Go!" Crista rasped.

Then she sped around the corner, just catching Cruz bent down at the shower trying to unwrap Rick. She had almost escaped when Rick shouted, "They're going!"

Cruz turned around. Crista froze. Her eyes met Cruz's. It felt as if everything drained out of her and she couldn't move. Rick shouted, "Get her!"

Something in Cruz's eyes told Crista to move, to go, to get out. Instantly, energy returned, and as if sprung from a trap, she leaped up the stairs. When she reached the top, she turned around and slammed the door shut. The key was still in it. She quickly rotated it until the lock snapped.

Lindy shouted behind her. "Help, Crista! It's Mr. Wilkins!" Mr. Wilkins had sagged over onto his side. He was tied up, and his head was bleeding. Obviously one of them, probably Rick, had struck him with something. Crista shook him, trying to wake him up. His eyelids twitched.

"Get a glass of water, Lindy."

The little girl ran into the bathroom. Crista worked at the knots, but they were too tight. Then she remembered the fishing knife. She took it out of her pocket, opened it, and cut the ropes. Mr. Wilkins was free.

Lindy ran back with the water. Crista poured it over his head, but he still didn't move. "Please wake up, Mr. Wilkins. Please!"

Waiting behind her, there was a sudden noise on the stairs. Then at the door.

Two loud bangs. They were trying to break down the door!

Mr. Wilkins's eyes popped open. He looked around. "Go for help," he wheezed, his voice scratchy. "Go for help!"

The banging on the door increased. Then there was a splintering crack.

"Go!" Mr. Wilkins cried.

Crista grabbed Lindy's hand. "We'll be back!" she yelled. They both fled to the front door. Looking back only once, they pushed it open. Just as they stepped through, they heard the basement door crack open.

·25·

There's No Way

"Through the woods!" Crista grabbed Lindy's hand, sure that Rick and Cruz would follow them in the truck along the road. They had to get to the Wilkinses' house. It was less than a quarter-mile down the road, but in a truck Rick and Cruz could get them. They had to go through the woods.

As they began to run, Crista knew their best chance was to split up. Once in the woods, she stopped and grabbed Lindy at the shoulders. "You have to go to the Wilkinses' without me, Lindy."

"But why?" Lindy was crying now and Crista could see she was more scared than she'd shown.

"I've got to divert Rick. Our best chance is for you to get to Mrs. Wilkins and have her call the police. I'm going..." Crista looked toward the road. She heard the truck roar in the yard, then screech out of the driveway and into the street.

"Go! Like the wind."

Lindy shook her head. "Not without you."

Crista gave her a push. "You have too. It's our only chance. I promise I'll be all right."

Wiping her eyes, Lindy sniffed, "Okay." She turned, sprinted 30 feet, then stopped.

"Go!" Crista yelled, watching her.

Lindy turned and ran. Crista could see she was committed now. "All right, Lord, keep him away from Lindy," Crista murmured. "Please!"

She saw the truck out at the road, cruising. It was Rick, peering into the woods. In the rear of the truck was the stereo equipment and the other things they had stolen. Crista figured Cruz must be guarding Mr. Wilkins.

Crista leaped out from behind the tree and began running parallel to him. He had to come after her. "Don't let him see Lindy," she said again out loud.

Suddenly, the truck turned into the trees.

He was driving into the woods in the truck! It was impossible.

Crista darted in and out among the trees, trying to think of what to do, where to go. She knew she had to get into denser woods where the truck couldn't follow. She ran breathless, her chest hammering, her face sweaty. Even in the cold air without a jacket she felt hot. She looked frantically around for trees, closer trees. Then she saw it up ahead—a clump.

The truck scooted and shimmied through the woods behind her, bumping up and down and knocking against trees and rocks. Some of the equipment fell out with a crash.

In 15 more seconds Crista reached a dense area and slowed down. Behind her, there was a loud crash. She turned around and saw the truck smashed up against a large rock. She watched a moment, wondering if Rick had been hurt.

But the door squeaked open and he jumped out. He yelled, "I'm gonna get you, girl. I'm gonna get you!"

He sprinted toward her. He didn't seem to have a weapon and Crista realized Cruz probably had the rifle to guard Mr. Wilkins. As she ran, ducking under branches and skirting around rocks, she silently prayed that Rick would trip and conk himself out again.

But he moved closer. She could hear him panting now, angry, cursing under his breath. She touched the fishing knife in her pocket, but she knew that was useless against him. She had to do something else. He was less than a hundred feet away.

She searched the woods, desperate for something, anything. He was going to catch her, but he had to know it was over by now. Lindy would be close to Mrs. Wilkins's house. The police would come. The truck was cracked up. What did Rick think he could do?

Her heart only hammered harder. She dodged in and out of trees. Rick was going to catch her if she didn't come up with some idea, and quick. He was only 50 feet away now, and gaining.

Then she saw them—the little yellow plastic strips. Mr. Wilkins's fox traps! He had laid out ten of them, in a line. Maybe, just maybe. She could see the top of the chicken coop ahead of her, maybe a hundred feet away.

She turned toward the traps. If she could just make it to the line.

Rick was closer now. "I've got you, you little..."

She pumped her legs harder, praying that she wouldn't strike a trap. Sweat dripped into her face. Her vision blurred. She couldn't see now. "Just make it past the traps," her mind shrieked.

She passed the first yellow ribbon. The traps were all hidden under leaves, a little piece of meat on the ground above them.

The second yellow ribbon.

He was only ten feet away. Her lungs burned. Behind her back she felt him reach out to her.

"Got you!" he yelled.

But he missed.

"Please, God!" she cried.

She didn't see the stone. Her toe caught it and she was flung headlong. She rolled, knowing he'd catch her in a moment. Instead, there was a scream. "Ahhhh!"

Then, "Owwww."

Crista rolled over and sat up. Rick's right foot was caught in one of the traps. And his left wrist was in another! He was sprawled out, pinned. He couldn't move!

She didn't wait. Getting up, she ran straight for the Wilkinses' house. She could now see the top of the farmhouse from the woods. And in the distance, she heard something else: a siren.

"Thank God," she whispered, and ran even faster.

·26·

An Important Talk

Crista arrived just in time to jump into the first cruiser and speed down to the Helstroms' house. Two other officers ran into the woods after Rick.

Four policemen were already at the house when Lindy and Crista arrived. Cruz was inside. He had the rifle at Mr. Wilkins's head. He was shouting and telling everyone to stay away from the house. One of the officers with a megaphone spoke to him from behind a cruiser. The officers had out their shotguns and pistols, all of them hidden behind the black-and-white cars.

Crista, Lindy, and Mrs. Wilkins ducked down behind one. One of the officers asked them about the layout of the house, where they could get in. Two men ran around back. Crista could see the house was surrounded. There was no way out. She was terrified for Mr. Wilkins. Mrs. Wilkins was crying hysterically and one of the men led her up the road to a waiting ambulance.

Listening to the radio in the police cruiser, Crista suddenly overheard it crackle, "SWAT team on the way. Helicopter. Prepare a landing area. Over."

"Roger. They can land on the road, no problem. Big area. Over."

159

"Eight minutes. Maybe less. Over."

The words seemed to ring in Crista's mind. *SWAT team.* SWAT team! They were going to shoot Cruz!

She gripped Lindy's shoulder as the policeman ordered, "You two go back to the ambulance. Stay down now and run fast."

"I'd like to stay here." Crista's concern for Cruz outweighed her fear.

"I'm sorry, Miss, you..."

"Please, we'll stay right behind the car. Mr. Wilkins ...Cruz... we're friends."

The policeman gazed at her with piercing green eyes. He was an older man. Crista remembered he was the chief of police in town. She had seen him on the streets and talked to him with her father. He always struck her as gentle and caring. He spoke in a friendly way. "You promise you won't stick your head up above the top of the car here?"

"We promise."

Lindy and Crista stooped behind the car. When Crista looked up into Lindy's eyes, she was still crying. "What are they going to do to Cruz if he doesn't give up?" Lindy asked.

"I don't know," Crista said.

"Will they shoot him?"

"I don't know."

"But they can't," Lindy cried.

"I know. Let's just hope and pray."

A few minutes later, Mr. and Mrs. Helstrom drove up and jumped out of the car. Lindy ran to them, and then Crista jumped up and hurried over, keeping down. They all stood by the ambulance.

Lindy was wailing, "Mommy, they're going to shoot Cruz. They're going to shoot him."

Mrs. Helstrom patted Lindy's back and tried to comfort her, but the little girl was adamant, "You have to stop them, Mommy. Cruz saved me. He saved my life. He doesn't mean to be bad. Not like Rick. He doesn't mean it."

Crista looked back at the police. There were two more cars now and several more men. The chief was still shouting through the bullhorn, and several men had donned bulletproof vests and helmets. No one had moved in yet, but Crista knew it was only a matter of time.

She couldn't let them shoot Cruz! Even if he was in there with a gun, he wouldn't hurt Mr. Wilkins. He was scared. If everyone would just calm down!

Overhead, there was a whirring sound. The leaves on the trees rustled, then flew around in a hurricane of wind. The helicopter looked huge. Everyone cowered under the downdraft. In ten seconds six men with high-powered rifles jumped out. In a crouch, they all ran for the police cars. The helicopter immediately lifted off. In another minute, all was silent. The chief was on the bullhorn again, warning Cruz that a SWAT team was in place. The six men looked like soldiers with their green flak jackets, helmets, and radio receivers plugged into their left ears.

This was worse, far worse. Okay, Cruz and Rick were wrong. But Rick was the bad one. Cruz was just— what? Tagging along. He didn't want to hurt anyone. He had saved Lindy! Saved her! Why couldn't anyone see that? He wasn't going to shoot anybody. He was just scared! Scared!

The men were in position, all around the house. Their rifles were up at their shoulders.

Crista stared at the house. She couldn't see Cruz or Mr. Wilkins now. They could be anywhere. She realized the policemen would probably break in through the basement or a side window. Plenty of movies showed SWAT teams doing just that kind of maneuver. Up the road, she spotted two officers leading Rick out of the woods and into a cruiser. So the bad guy was finally caught.

Crista turned back to the scene. Lindy was still wailing that her father and mother couldn't let them shoot Cruz. Suddenly, without thinking about the danger, Crista began walking across toward the police. When she reached the car, Lindy broke away and ran toward her. Immediately, there was a commotion, policemen running around shouting to Lindy to keep down. Mr. and Mrs. Helstrom sped after her and grabbed her just as she reached the car.

"Don't shoot him! Please don't shoot him!" Crista begged the policeman. "Please. Cruz is not a bad person."

"I'm sorry, but we have to move in. We know how to handle our work here. If you would all just go over by the ambulance ..."

"Please," Crista was insistent. "Just let me and Lindy talk to him. He saved Lindy's life. He'll listen. I know he will."

"You're a minor, Miss, I'm sorry. Now please ..."

"He's not a killer!" Crista shouted. "Please, just let us talk to him. We won't even go up to the house. We'll just stand here behind the cars, and we'll talk on the thing—the megaphone thing. Please. Just let me try. *Please.* It won't hurt anything."

Lindy was quiet behind her. Crista looked into the chief's quiet eyes. He suddenly motioned to one of the men behind him. "All right," he gruffly agreed. "I'll give you one minute. Is that understood? And you are not to go out in front of the car. You are not to approach the building in any way. Is that understood?"

Crista nodded.

"Okay. I'm going to have you put on a bulletproof vest, just in case. It'll be kind of big, but I think you should put it on."

"What about Lindy?"

He looked at the little girl. "All right. Her, too."

An officer helped Crista put on a vest, and then Lindy. Finally, the chief gave Crista the bullhorn. He showed her how to operate it. Then he said, "Just be calm, okay?"

"Okay."

Her knees shaking, Crista stood. Suddenly, her mouth was dry, her heart pounding, and she had no idea what to say. For a moment, she hesitated. But she felt Lindy's grip on her hand and silently she prayed. Then she began, "Cruz, this is Crista."

She paused. "Cruz, you don't have to say anything. Lindy and I just want to say this."

Struggling for the words, nothing would seem to come into her mind, but she pressed on. "Cruz, there are a lot of people out here with guns. And they—" Lindy squeezed Crista's hand.

"Cruz, we don't want to see you get hurt. Lindy and me. None of us. Please, Cruz, listen. Please give up and come out. Please. Lindy's right here with me. Rick is caught and the truck is cracked up. So please listen. They will shoot you. And we don't want you to... to..." Crista couldn't say it.

Lindy tugged on Crista's arm. "The cookies." she whispered. "Remember the cookies."

Crista breathed out heavily. "Cruz, remember the cookies we brought you? And remember how you saved Lindy? You're not like this. I know it. You're not. Please don't make them have to shoot you."

The chief touched Crista's shoulder and she stooped back down. He said, "You did well. I'm sorry."

He started to turn to the other men and nod.

But the front door suddenly opened. Mr. Wilkins yelled, "Don't shoot. It's me. I have Cruz's gun. He's giving up. Don't shoot."

Mr. Wilkins threw the rifle out onto the lawn, then he stepped out into the light. He walked slowly onto the porch, then down the steps. When he was still on the sidewalk, Cruz appeared in shadow of the door. He walked out, his head down, his hands up.

Seconds later, the policemen surrounded him and put the handcuffs on his wrists. As he was led away, Crista caught his eyes. He smiled slightly, then said, "Thanks."

·27·
Big Questions

It didn't take long for the incident to hit the news. Lindy was interviewed. Crista was interviewed. There were reporters and policemen and people all over the Helstroms' house. Even Dr. Mayfield drove over and they gathered in the living room with the Wilkins to talk to the reporters.

When it was over, Lindy asked Crista, "Do you think we can go see Cruz? He might feel better. He didn't want to hurt us. I know he didn't." She was crying and Crista could see Lindy really felt for Cruz as much as she did.

Crista promised to ask her father about it. She still wasn't sure how she felt about the whole ordeal. She thought at first she should feel angry, like she even hated them, especially Rick. But deep down, she didn't. She felt sorry for them. Maybe if they'd really injured someone she'd feel differently. She knew what they had done was wrong, and if she and Lindy hadn't escaped, several people could have been seriously hurt. But Cruz, she knew, hadn't wanted to hurt anyone. Maybe he hadn't even wanted to steal.

While none of that excused what had happened, somehow Crista wanted to tell Rick and Cruz she did not hate them. She realized it might not even matter to

Rick, but what about Cruz? He had saved Lindy's life. He had always tried to be nice. He had argued with Rick about the whole heist. He wasn't all bad.

Rick, though. Rick was another matter. She didn't know whether she could ever be nice to him again, or even look at him. He might have hurt both Lindy and her badly. Even as she thought about it, she shuddered.

All evening, she struggled with the idea. She was reluctant to talk to her father about it, but finally that night she sat down in the living room and said, "Daddy, can I talk to you about something?"

He put down his paper and grinned. "Little old me? After all this fame and attention?"

"Dad-deeeee!"

"Okay, what's on your mind?"

"Do you think it would be right to visit Cruz in jail?"

Her father gazed at her a long time before he answered. He finally asked, "Why?"

Immediately, Crista felt uncomfortable. She was never good with that question, even with Lindy. "I don't know," she answered. "I just think it would be right. I don't want him to think I hate him."

He seemed to be thinking. "Well, I guess I would not be against it, so long as you did not go into the cell or put yourself in danger. I'd be glad to go down with you."

"Would you?"

"Sure, after I get home from the hospital. I guess it's really the kind of thing I think God would want you to do."

"You do?"

Again, he stopped to think. "Well, we don't just stop caring about someone because they do something wrong, even something very wrong. Those two men could have hurt you and Lindy and Mr. Wilkins badly, Crista. You do realize that?"

She looked down at her lap. "Yes."

"And what they had been doing was very evil."

"I know." Crista noticed her heart bumping inside her chest. She didn't want to look at her father's face. She could feel his eyes on her.

He said, "But if you want to extend to them forgiveness and compassion, I would not tell you not to. I think that's what following Jesus is all about."

She looked up, almost surprised. "You do?"

"Of course."

She knew he was right. But her dad had referred to "them," and she meant only Cruz. Rick had always been mean. He had never even tried to be nice, except when he got something he wanted.

She could feel her father's eyes still on her. When she looked up, he gazed into her eyes with a directness she hadn't seen in a long time. "Crista," he said, "I know you want to visit Cruz. But what about Rick?"

Looking away, Crista murmured, "I don't know."

"It's hard, isn't it?"

She nodded.

He stood and walked over to the sofa. He put his hand on her leg. "Crissie, I know it's difficult. But though you may not like Rick, and though he did wrong, more wrong than Cruz, if you go to that jail, you can't offer forgiveness and compassion to Cruz and not to Rick."

"But Rick will just spit on it, Daddy."

Her father's face looked soft and understanding in the firelight. "Yes, he might. You never know what he might do. But you still should offer it, even if he spits on it. That's how God treats us. How Jesus does. That's what Jesus did with the very people who nailed Him to the cross."

She looked up into his kind blue eyes. "You mean when He forgave them?"

"Yes."

She knew instantly her dad was right. It was what she'd been struggling to do—to love people who mistreated you, even hated you. Like Autumn in Lindy's class. And now Rick. She said, "Maybe I should not go at all."

Her father shrugged slightly. "You don't have to. No one will fault you for not going. But you want to, don't you?"

She nodded. "I want to tell Cruz."

"If you go, you'll see Rick."

"I know."

"Then you should be prepared."

"For what?"

"Not to hate him. And to forgive him if he asks. And maybe even if he doesn't ask."

"I don't know, Daddy."

"Well, pray about it and think about it. Maybe God will help you see what you need to do."

"Okay."

She thought about it all night. Shortly before she fell asleep, though, she knew what the right thing to do was. She had to offer that forgiveness. For Cruz's sake. And Lindy's. And Rick's.

She thought about it a little longer. Then she realized she had to do it for her sake, too.

·28·
The Jail

The next day at school, Lindy and Crista were true heroines. Everybody seemed to know about what happened and wanted to know more. For once, Lindy was the real center of attention in her class. Even Autumn was impressed. Lindy stood about in her glory, but whenever she saw Crista she always asked, "Do you think we can go see Cruz?"

That afternoon on the way home from school, Crista said, "All right, Lindy, I think we should go see them. But we can't make them think what they did was okay."

"Yeah, but we can tell them we still like them, especially Cruz."

Crista smiled. "Then let's bake some cookies and see if we can take them down. My dad said he'd drive us tonight, if we want."

"Excellent!"

They made a batch of chocolate chip cookies with big chunks of broken up dark chocolate in them instead of just the usual chips. That night Dr. Mayfield took them both down to the jail before dinner with two plates of cookies covered in aluminum foil. At the police station, the officer, one of the men Crista had seen at the Helstroms' house, frisked them all and

169

checked the cookies. He even asked for one, and Lindy gladly obliged, saying, "Crista makes the best cookies. She could start a store."

He chomped into it and chortled, "I believe you. I'd buy 'em."

He led them through a door into a back room with four cells. Cruz and Rick were in different ones, catty-cornered so that Rick's cell was first. He looked up a moment when Crista, Lindy, and Dr. Mayfield walked in, then stared back at his feet glumly. Crista stopped with Lindy at the cell. "We brought you some cookies, Rick," Crista said, her heart pounding worse than it had when Rick was chasing her.

"Yeah, with huge chocolate chips," Lindy added. "To show you we're not mad."

Rick squinted at them with an evil, hateful eye. "I'm not talking to you. Bug off."

Crista swallowed and glanced at her dad who nodded encouragement. She pushed the little plate under the opening at the bottom of the cell. "In case you change..."

Jumping up and kicking the plate so that the cookies flew everywhere, Rick shouted, "I don't want you to be nice to me! Understand? None of you. So go away."

Crista and Lindy fell back, genuinely afraid. Dr. Mayfield stared at Rick angrily. "Young man..." he began.

Rick glared at him. "You shut up, too. I don't want to hear from any of you. Got it?"

"You don't have to be mean about it," Lindy suddenly said shrilly. "We're not mad at you and you were gonna hurt us and Mr. Wilkins."

"Get out of here!"

Cruz watched the scene from the next cell. He said quietly, "Maybe if we would have listened to them before, we wouldn't be in this mess, Rick."

"You shut up, too, you coward!" Rick sat back down and stared out the back window through the bars.

Crista stooped down, trying to pick up what was left of the cookies and putting them back on the plate. She was so scared, she thought her whole body was shaking.

The two girls stepped over to Cruz's cell, with Dr. Mayfield still looking at Rick. Squaring off a moment, Rick sat back down, angry, his face dark and taut with hatred.

As they stepped up to the cell, Cruz said, "I'm sorry. I'm really sorry, Crista. Both of you. I . . ." His eyes teared, and he shook his head angrily. His dark hair was in his eyes, and he hadn't shaved. He looked scared. "I'm sorry. I'm completely, everlastingly sorry."

Crista and Lindy took one hand each. Lindy smiled at him, "Crista and I promise to bring you cookies every day. As many as you want. Even if Rick doesn't want us to, we're gonna. Crista's gonna start a store."

Cruz looked at Crista inquiringly, but Crista laughed, "Lindy, I'm not going to start a store. Good grief."

"I'd buy them," Lindy asserted confidently. "They have the biggest pieces of chocolate in them ever. Ever!"

Cruz smiled and shook his head. "This is more than enough." He looked into Crista's eyes, then blinked away. He spoke in a low voice, almost choking, "I'm sorry, Crista. I wouldn't have hurt anyone. I didn't want to. I swear."

Rick snorted noisily across the way, but Cruz looked first at Crista and then at Lindy and finally at Dr.

Mayfield. "I know we did wrong. It was stupid, and I deserve whatever I get. I just hope you'll . . ." He wiped his eyes.

"We forgive you," Crista said softly, squeezing his hand.

"I do, too," Lindy quickly added. "You saved my life and I'll tell everyone. Everyone. I'll tell them all what you did."

Cruz calmed down and smiled. "Thanks. But I think this is gonna be bad."

Crista felt braver now. "God'll help you, Cruz. If you believe in Him. I know He will. And there's something else."

Cruz looked up into her eyes.

"When you didn't come after me in the basement, I knew then, right then, that you really, honestly cared about us and didn't want to hurt us. Even when Rick shouted at you."

"I'm sorry I even thought about it."

"It's all right. You didn't do the wrong others wanted you to do, and that's what counts."

He shook his head. "Not where I'm going."

"God can help you, Cruz. I know it."

"Yeah, my mom and dad believed like that. I guess even I did at one time. But people always said I'd turn out bad. I guess they were right."

Lindy picked up a cookie. "Here, Cruz, eat one. It'll make you feel better."

Leaning back while hanging onto the bars, Cruz looked at them with amazement, "You all crack me up. I can't believe you really came to visit us."

Suddenly, Rick stood up in the next cell. "This is making me sick! Cruz has turned into crybaby." He paused. "Will you all cut with the religious stuff and get out of here?"

"They're just being nice, Rick," Cruz answered angrily. "What don't you shut up for once?"

"You're the one who doesn't get it!" Lindy shouted.

Rick kicked the bars and threw the little bench he had been sitting on across the cell. It glanced off the bars, with a loud clang. The noise echoed on the walls, and the policeman came back through the door. "Hey, you," he shouted. "Tone it down in there, or we'll put you in solitary."

"It would be better than this church service here," Rick raged.

"One more crack like that and you're gone. You understand that?" the policeman said. He looked at Dr. Mayfield and Crista and Lindy. "You all okay?"

"Yes," Dr. Mayfield said and Crista nodded. Lindy added, "He's just all mad, as usual. He's always mad."

"You got that right," the policeman said. He scowled at Rick, then closed the door again. Dr. Mayfield told the girls, "All right, girls, say goodbye now. We've got to go."

Crista slid both plates of cookies into Cruz's cell. "If Rick changes his mind."

Rick sneered, "I'm not changin' my mind."

Cruz frowned, but he said to Crista and Lindy, "Thanks for coming. I won't let you down again. I promise."

His lanky hair looked greasy so Crista asked, "Do you need a comb or anything?"

Immediately, Cruz ran his fingers through it. "No. I got my stuff. They brought it in after they searched our place." He smiled. "I haven't been thinking about good grooming at the moment." He shrugged. "Anyway, thanks for coming. Really. You don't know how much it means."

Crista gazed into Cruz's flinching dark eyes. Stirring up her courage one more time, she said, "Can we pray for you?"

There was a long pause. Rick snorted with sarcasm again, then shook his head and looked away. But Cruz nodded, "Yeah, pray that I won't end up a complete bad guy."

"We will." Crista looked at Lindy and she nodded. For a moment they bowed their heads and Crista prayed briefly. She started to look up after saying Amen, but Lindy suddenly broke in, "And please, Jesus, tell Cruz You love him. And tell Rick, too, even if he doesn't want to hear it."

Rick laughed raucously in his cell. "This takes the cake, man."

When they finished, Crista gave Cruz's hand one more squeeze. "We'll come again, I promise."

"Thanks."

They turned up the aisle. Dr. Mayfield stood at the end, waiting. Crista did not even want to look at Rick. As she and Lindy started toward the exit, they kept to the opposite side. Crista's heart felt like it was in her mouth. All she heard was the pounding. They reached the front of Rick's cell. He hadn't moved. He was glaring at them as they sidled by.

Crista forced one foot ahead of another. Suddenly, Rick shouted and leaped at them. He banged into the bars, but both hands shot through.

He didn't touch them, but Crista and Lindy tore forward until they landed in Dr. Mayfield's arms. Rick laughed, a piercing, cold, heartless laugh. They all went through the door and as it closed behind them, Rick was still laughing.

Outside, Dr. Mayfield shook his head, "I shouldn't have let you come. I'm sorry. I shouldn't have let you come here."

But Crista objected immediately, "No. I'm okay."

"Me, too," Lindy added.

Dr. Mayfield looked at them, a smile coming onto his face. "You're really all right?"

"It wasn't as bad as I thought.."

He stooped slightly, looking into both of their eyes. "I'm proud of you two. You know that, don't you?"

Crista and Lindy almost leaped into his arms and he enclosed them for a moment. Crista began to cry, but Lindy said, "He's not so bad. I'm not scared of him."

Moments later, they were on the road back to home. Everyone was quiet. When they reached Lindy's house, the little girl jumped out and turned to Crista, "You are starting a store."

Crista laughed. "For you, Lindy—anything."

She led Crista up to the door of the house, and Mrs. Helstrom met them, relieved Lindy was back so soon. She smiled, "We're finally getting this place cleaned up."

Not knowing what else to say, Crista gave Lindy a quick kiss. "See you tomorrow at school."

Lindy watched as she walked back out to the car.

Crista and her father drove home, and across the wide front seat of the station wagon, his hand touched hers. "I'm very proud of you, Crista. Very proud. That was a courageous thing you did in there."

Crista smiled but her eyes were sad. "I just wish Rick wasn't so hateful."

"You can't make him change, honey."

"But I wish I could."

"I know. We all do."

The next day Lindy and Crista were still the talk of the school. Lindy was riding the crest of a tidal wave, and Crista thought she couldn't possibly get any higher.

But that afternoon Lindy pranced on the bus, full of new excitement.

"Guess what?" she said as she sat down next to Crista and Jeff.

"I don't know, what?" Jeff played along.

Lindy opened her backpack and unrolled the caricature Crista had done more than a month before. "It was in my desk!" Lindy exclaimed.

"Who put it there?" Crista asked.

"Don't know. But I have a pretty good guess." Lindy grinned widely.

Crista smiled. "Someone who may be a friend from now on."

"Yep," Lindy said happily. "I have more friends now than I can count!"

As the bus headed out, Crista thought about how quickly things changed in the world, and many times for the better. "People can be so neat," she murmured.

"What?" Lindy gave her a quizzical look.

"Oh nothing," Crista answered. "Just thinking how great today is."

"Yeah," Lindy nodded her head enthusiastically. "Me, too. And I can't wait for tomorrow!"